"POOR CHILD, POOR CHILD." HE STROKED HER HAIR GENTLY.

Then, his hand fell on her bare shoulder. "So soft," he muttered, "skin so soft . . ." Putting his finger under her chin, he tilted her face toward the candle flame. "Lovely girl, so lovely." He ran his finger under her eyes. "Tears—mus' not cry. Do not like to see you cry."

She sniffed and sniffed again but the gentleness with which he had addressed her only brought more tears, and not wanting him to see them, she buried her head amidst the cushions. He put his arm around her and though his grasp was tight, she was not afraid. She had seen his face, haloed by a mist of tears and though she would have been hard put to describe them, she had found his features to her liking and also, it seemed to her that warmth and kindness radiated from him.

"There . . . there, poor little one," he murmured, patting her shoulder. Stretching out on the cushions beside her, he pulled her against him so that her head lay near his heart and she could hear its steady beat beneath her ear.

She did not push him away . . .

Novels by
Zabrina Faire

Lady Blue
The Midnight Match
Enchanting Jenny
The Romany Rebel
The Wicked Cousin
Athena's Airs
Bold Pursuit
Pretty Kitty

Published by
WARNER BOOKS

Your Warner Library of Regency Romance

Pretty Kitty

Zabrina Faire

WARNER BOOKS

A Warner Communications Company

WARNER BOOKS EDITION

Copyright © 1981 by Florence Stevenson
All rights reserved.

Cover art by Walter Popp

Warner Books, Inc., 75 Rockefeller Plaza, New York, N.Y. 10019

Ⓦ A Warner Communications Company

Printed in the United States of America

First Printing: February, 1981

10 9 8 7 6 5 4 3 2 1

One

Miss Kitty Maynard of The Oaks sat in a swing attached to a tall oak, one of the many on the plantation which were the inspiration for its name. She put her small bare toes to the ground and pushed. In her estimation, swinging was the only effective way to bring up a breeze.

In all of her eighteen years and two months, she had not experienced heat of the intensity of that which lay over Virginia in this August of 1814. The trees and foliage seemed to waver as if viewed from behind a screen of water and a great quiet prevailed—as if the insects, animals, and birds were too warm to go about their normal business. Yet, though her exertions were causing her thin white muslin gown to cling to her body as if she had dampened it purposely, which had been the fashion when she was little, she continued to pump with both feet until she was off the ground and high enough to glimpse in the distance, the diminished flag that flew on the roof of Heathlands, the home of her fiancé.

"*Robert,*" Kitty whispered yearningly. To think of Robert Heath of Heathlands was to arouse an instant image of him—tall, slender, aquiline of countenance, dressed in a neat black suit, beautifully arranged cravat, the stiff high collar of his shirt accentuating the proud way he held his head, his dark brown hair carefully coiffed—the very picture of a rising young diplomat and member of Mr. Madison's staff.

Kitty smiled with pride. Everyone said that Robert was bound to make a name for himself. Yet to think of him was not always to see that Robert. That image could easily be displaced by another younger Robert: smaller, freckled, not so soberly garbed, riding with her through the lanes that ran from The Oaks to Heathlands. There were even earlier memories, for she had known him all her life. In fact, she reflected with a smile: she had known him when she could not *remember* knowing him—when he, a rambunctious three-year-old visiting her nursery with his mama, had given her cradle a push that had nearly overturned it. It had brought him a slap from Jael, her mother's servant, followed by an outburst of rage from Mrs. Heath, who had told her mama that the slave ought to be whipped for raising her hand against him.

Mama, who had related the incident to her more than once, still waxed indignant over it. "I told her that I would never hurt anybody under my protection. Oh, I do not like that woman. You mark my words—you and Robert had better build your home on the other side of the Blue Ridge mountains else she will rule the roost!"

That, of course, was impossible. Kitty knew she could never pry Robert from Heathlands. Furthermore, she did not actually want to. She loved Fairfax County.

She could not imagine living anywhere else. Thanks to her father's Will, she owned half of The Oaks and would have the whole of it upon her mother's death. Her mouth tightened at the thought. It had been terrible losing papa two years ago; she could not bear to think of anything happening to her mama—and it could, for she was not strong ... and having another baby at her age! The swing had been slowing down and thinking of that baby, she gave herself another hefty push and blinked tears away.

"I feel like Hamlet," she murmured. " 'The funeral baked meats did furnish forth the wedding feast ...' "

That, of course, was not quite accurate. It had been a year though it had not seemed nearly so long and her mama, no sooner doffing her widow's weeds than she was in bridal attire, walking up the aisle of the Presbyterian church with her hand on Wellington Abbott's arm. Wellington Abbott, who was surely the satyr to papa's hyperion, she thought, recalling Keats's poem. She could not understand why her mother had found him so charming. She knew that Jael did not, and recalled a morning almost a year ago ...

"Don' like a man what smile wif his mouf an' frown wif his eyes." Jael had a great deal more to say about Wellington Abbott—but only to Kitty. For Kitty, she had advice as well. "I wouldn' criticize that man to yo' mama, honey. She don' like the people she loves not to love each other. You know that."

"But I don't see how she could love him," a mutinous and grieving Kitty cried.

"Don' see it myse'f, but she ain' happy alone. She needs a man."

"She had papa."

"Yo' papa's dead. Supposin' yo' Robert was to up an' die?"

"Oh, don't!" Kitty had protested.

"Wouldn' *you* feel lonely?"

"If Robert died, I wouldn't ever want anybody else."

Jael gave Kitty what mama called her "sphinx look." "That's what you say now . . . but you'd understand yo' mama better if you was older."

"I don't see what *older* has to do with it," seventeen-year-old Kitty retorted.

She was older now and she still did not understand. A year of having Wellington Abbott as her stepfather and living under the same roof with him had been terrible. However, it would have been worse if he had taken mama to live at his plantation way off in Carroll County. She shook her head. No use to think about him any more than was absolutely necessary. It was bad enough seeing him every day and having to listen to his attempts at being her papa—trying to lay down the law about her riding bareback and going swimming in the creek that ran through the lower end of the property. She blushed. When he had caught her swimming, she had had to hide in the reeds until he had stepped away from the bank . . . and his eyes! A man married to her mama had no business looking at her like that. She was not sure how she would define his gaze but certainly there had been something horrid about it.

"Umph." Kitty suddenly clutched the ropes of her swing as a sudden push from behind sent it up high and wobbling. As it came back she heard laughter behind her. Turning her head, she glared down on a tall, muscular young man with a shock of pale yellow hair and very pale blue eyes—white eyes, Jael called them. "Twice as big an' twice as mean as his brother," she had muttered when she had first seen him.

"Rayburn Abbott!" Kitty gasped indignantly while

the swing slowed to a stop. "You could have made me break my neck!"

"You were holding on tight, else I wouldn't have done it," he drawled. "I wouldn't ever want to hurt that pretty little neck, Kitty May."

"Don't call me Kitty May—I don't like it. Why are you here? I thought you were tending Abbott's Ford."

"Thought I'd come up and see how Wellington's doin'. And see how you were doin', too. Very well, I'd say—an' lookin' prettier'n ever. 'Specially to a man who likes green eyes an' red hair. Fifty years or so ago, they'd have it red-haired lasses were witches. I'd say you were bewitchin'."

"And I'd say you'd best remember that I am betrothed to Robert Heath."

"I remember." He grinned. "He's not man enough for you, my pretty. Let's hope the British get him afore he's much older."

"Don't talk like that," she retorted sharply. "Nothing's going to happen to Robert."

"Nothin' he don't have comin' to him." He shrugged. "One of these days, Kitty May, you're goin' to have the scales drop off those pretty green eyes an' you're goin' to see Mr. Robert Prissy-Pants Heath the way he really is. For your sake I hope it's afore you've wedded him."

She jumped down from the swing. "I am not going to stay here and listen to you insult Robert. You've not met him a dozen times in your life!"

"That's right and I'm glad of it. Stuck-up humbug. You need a real man, Kitty May." He suddenly made a grab for her.

"Don't you come near me, Rayburn Abbott!" she cried indignantly and fled through the trees in the direction of the house.

"Barefoot like a field han' and runnin' in this kind of weather. Mus' have taken leave of yo' senses, that's what."

Jael, a tall ebony-skinned woman, dressed all in white, even to the turban that emphasized her resemblance to an Egyptian sphinx, bent a censorious eye on Kitty, while she gently anointed her temples with witch-hazel.

Kitty, lying panting on her bed, said, "He's here again . . . Rayburn."

Jael frowned. "Him . . . why's *he* here?"

"To see his brother." She detailed the incident by the swing.

"That's the Abbotts for you," sniffed Jael. "Sneakin' about in the woods like cattle thieves. I wish Mr. Robert was home. He wouldn't come pesterin' you then."

"Oh, so do I. Julie Pickett went up to Washington on Monday. I wanted to go with her but mama—well, you know how she worries and Wellington said I wasn't to go." She frowned. "Not that I would have paid any mind to him . . . but with mama breeding . . ."

"It ain't safe up Washington way. Not with them Redcoats camped all about."

"Robert wrote that they wouldn't march on Washington." Kitty heaved a long sigh. "I'd feel safe if I were with him. Much safer than here. I think I'd almost prefer a Redcoat to Rayburn Abbott. And he'll be staying to supper. I wish I could say I was taken sick."

"An' leave yo' mama to cope with them two big he-goats? I hope you have more consideration than that, Miz Kitty."

"If mama didn't want to cope with them, she shouldn't have married Wellington Abbott," Kitty told her bitterly, *"and"*—she looked Jael in the eye—"I am eighteen now and I still don't understand why she had to have him around the house. It's half my house. If I had my way, I'd draw a line right down the middle and bar him from setting foot in—"

"I do believe the sun's made you light-headed, Miz Kitty. You rest so's you'll be sweet an' pert for supper," Jael interrupted and before Kitty could say anything else, she had glided from the room.

"Sweet an' pert for supper!" Kitty pounded a pillow. "I don't care what she says. I am not going to sit at table and face Rayburn Abbott across the flowers. I am going to sleep until morning!"

In the small octagonal room which Adeline Abbott preferred to use when just family was present, supper was drawing to a close. Kitty, resenting the suggestion that Rayburn be considered part of the family, had kept her eyes on her plate as much as she dared, not even raising them to glance at her mother, for as often as she did, she encountered Rayburn's pale stare. He was seated directly across from her with Wellington Abbott to her left and her mama to her right, but due to the small size of the circular table they were far too near to each other for her peace of mind.

Whenever she did look up, she quickly fastened her eyes on her mother, and each time she felt a pang. Adeline Abbott did not look well: there were dark shadows under her eyes and her skin which had been a creamy white when she had wed Wellington Abbott, was now a pale yellow; where her figure was not increasing, she was painfully thin. Resentment flooded through Kitty. Mama should not have had this child. She was thirty-nine-years old and not strong—she had never been strong. Furthermore, if there had been other children, they should have been born when papa was alive. She wondered why it had not happened. It was a great mystery, even to the doctor.

"Kitty, you're mighty quiet tonight. Cat got your tongue?" Wellington Abbott said, breaking a short silence.

Kitty turned cold eyes on her stepfather. He was better-looking than his brother, but she could not abide his sharp, foxy features. She said, "I was thinking."

"The dinner table's a place for conversation, not thinking," he remarked with a smile that revealed his sharp white teeth—fox's teeth, Kitty thought.

"I had the impression it was for eating," she said.

"You don't eat enough to keep a bird alive." Rayburn grinned. "I expect I could span your waist with my thumb and forefinger."

"You are too thin, Kitty." Adeline's look was anxious as it rested on her daughter.

Kitty was annoyed. What she had tried to avoid all evening had come to pass; the conversation was centering upon her. She said, "I am eating as much as I ever did, Mama." She turned her attention back to her plate and took a mouthful of pudding, hoping that the talk would veer in another direction so that she would not be forced to look up again.

Her mother, however, stubbornly kept to the subject. "I guess you're missing Robert."

"Yes, I do miss him." Kitty darted a glance at Rayburn as she made this admission. She expected to see mocking laughter in his white eyes but instead found them curiously intent, fastened upon her with a speculative look which made her very uncomfortable, though she could not have said why.

"Well, my dear, I expect when the trouble's over, he'll come home for a spell." Adeline added softly, "He and his mother . . . imagine her going up to Washington at a time like this! Well, Evadne always did have more than her share of gumption. You have to say that about her. I guess that comes from being a general's lady."

"From what I understand, she could have been and maybe should've been the general herself," Wellington Abbott said.

"How can you understand anything about her?" Kitty flashed. "You don't know her."

"Kitty, dear," Adeline murmured.

"I don't need to know her," he returned, evidently unperturbed by what might have been construed as rudeness on the part of his stepdaughter. "Word gets around."

Kitty had the definite impression that rather than pointing a finger at Mrs. Heath, he was aiming some manner of subtle criticism in the direction of her son. She longed to answer him back but since he had said nothing she could challenge, she had perforce to remain silent. Therefore, she was extremely relieved when her mother suddenly rose, saying with her pretty and slightly conciliating smile, "I expect it's time we left the gentlemen to their port. Come into the music room and play for me, Kitty, my love."

Kitty rose at once and as she did, she caught a look that flashed between the two men. Though she was hard put to understand why, it made her very uneasy. It was amazing, she thought resentfully, how when they were together, they always managed to destroy her peace of mind. Indeed, she almost felt menaced by the pair, though that, of course, was ridiculous. Thanks to her father's unusual Will, she was independently wealthy and, in common with her mother, part-mistress of The Oaks, as well as Robert's affianced bride. There was no way they could touch her. Still, she wished she had gone to Washington with Julie Pickett and remembered again that

Wellington had forbidden it. In remaining behind she had, she thought uncomfortably, acknowledged that he did have some manner of jurisdiction over her. That had been a very grave error and one that must be rectified immediately, though she was uncertain how this could best be effected. With a little sigh, she followed her mama down the hall.

The Music Room at The Oaks was singularly restful, particularly at night when the candles were lit in the sconces that adorned its pale green walls. In arched niches at either end of the room were marble statues of Orpheus with his harp and Apollo playing on his lyre. The ceiling was painted to represent Parnassus with the nine muses wandering through the pillared temple. Its four windows faced the garden which was of course dark when Kitty and her mother came in; the one to sit down at the small square Erard piano imported from Germany by her music-loving grandfather, the other to sink down upon the chaise-longue, gratefully resting her head upon cushions covered in a pale green velvet to match the draperies at the windows.

Kitty regarded her mother anxiously. "You do not seem at all the thing this evening, Mama."

"It's the strain," Adeline said plaintively. "You know I never could abide strife . . . my nerves . . . and at this time, Kitty, when I am increasing. It makes it doubly hard when you sit there at table being so unkind to your papa and your uncle."

Kitty's eyes widened in indignation. "My papa! My uncle!" she repeated. "Why—what can you mean, Mama? They're no kin of mine!"

"Well, they are, Kitty since I married Mr. Abbott, and there's not a day passes that you don't contrive to make him feel as if he weren't welcome in this house. Why, you were downright sullen at supper." Tears stood

14

in Adeline's eyes. "And it hurts me, it really does. It hurts Mr. Abbott, too, though he'd never say a word against you."

Kitty felt a whole stream of words against Mr. Abbott come welling up from her throat ready to pour out, ready to demand how her mother could possibly imagine that Kitty could like anyone as sly as her stepfather or as horrid and insinuating as Rayburn Abbott, especially after she had known and loved her own papa! However, the thought of the late Samuel Maynard served as a check to those hot words. A vivid image of her parents together in this very room arose in her mind—Adeline lying on her chaise-longue while Kitty played the piano, accompanying her father on his violin. For a moment she could actually hear the strains of the instrument playing Mozart's Sonata in E-Flat Major, which had been one of their favorites. Unconsciously her fingers responded to that phantom melody and she began to play the accompaniment.

"Kitty," Adeline said sharply, "we've not done speaking. I marvel at your rudeness."

Kitty took her hands from the keyboard. "I am sorry, Mama, I was thinking of papa and how we used to play here together of an evening."

"Ohhhh." To her surprise, her mother threw both hands over her face. "You are reproaching me for being unfaithful to him, but—but he's dead and I can't shut myself in his coffin nor immolate myself upon a pyre as they say Indian widows do." Her shoulders shook with sobs. "I shouldn't think you'd begrudge me this new happiness, Kitty."

Kitty sighed. All her life she had known her mother to be gentle, sweet and dependent. Her father had admired this last quality, mainly because it had been something he had not known at home. His own mother had been an indomitable lady who during the Revolution had kept a rifle and two pistols in readiness in case of marauding Redcoats and used them to such good effect that she had killed a lieutenant and a major who had come to commandeer her horses. Kitty had loved to hear tales of her grandmother, but Adeline had shuddered over them —which, of course, had also pleased him. It was a pity he had increased Adeline's penchant for clinging to his shoulder, for she had found it all too necessary to find another shoulder. However, there being nothing her daughter could do about it now, Kitty said carefully, "I don't begrudge you, your . . . happiness, Mama, not in the least."

Adeline did not seem to hear her. "I do miss Sam," she said. "I think about him a great deal, a very great deal—but he's gone. You've got to remember that too, Kitty."

"I do remember it, Mama."

"Times change . . . lives change," Adeline mused. "Things you don't expect to happen, happen, like the British."

"The British, Mama?"

"This war. I was five years old when the Revolution ended, but I can remember all the rejoicing we did because the Redcoats were driven from our shores. Nobody expected they'd be back, but they are, and we might be burned out of our home, and I am expecting a baby! Oh, it's not to be tolerated. I don't know what I shall do!"

"Mama." Kitty rose from the piano to kneel beside her mother's couch. "Please don't take on like that. You're only borrowing trouble. There's no reason to suppose the British will march through here."

"I can't help but be troubled! That's why, when I can still have a little peace . . . please, Kitty dear, for my sake, try to love Mr. Abbott and his brother. I cannot bear the people of whom I am the fondest to be at odds with each other. And Mr. Abbott feels that way, too. I know your attitude is disturbing to him. Oh, I do miss him so dreadfully! Sam could always drop oil upon the troubled waters."

Listening to this strangely disconnected speech, Kitty's heart went out to her mother. For the first time, it was obvious to her that Adeline was still grieving for her late husband. Yet she also realized and regretfully that it was not the grief of a mature woman but that of a confused child. She had, she recalled, always felt older than her mother—never more than now when she knew she must alleviate that confusion, not add to it. "Mama, Mama!" She grasped her mother's thin hands. "I will do my best to be pleasant to Mr. Abbott and Rayburn."

"Oh?" Adeline's lovely smile brightened her tear-washed countenance. "You will, Kitty? Honest and truly?"

"Honest and truly, Mama," her daughter sighed. "Now what would you like to hear me play?"

"Anything you choose, dearest. Perhaps the Fantasy in C Minor by Mozart. Your papa loves . . . loved the way you played it. I expect I should like to hear that."

Hours later in her own chamber, Kitty, sitting in front of her dressing table while Becky Lou, her personal maid, brushed out her long red locks, stared into the mirror, not seeing her face but the music room, invaded by Wellington Abbott and his brother. Mozart had been banished mid-bar as her stepfather had laughingly demanded a ditty from *Love in a Village*. Obedient to her promise, Kitty had dutifully obliged, with Rayburn to turn the pages since she was not familiar with the music. He had stood far closer to her than necessary to perform this task; and, as she played, she had glanced past him once

17

to meet her stepfather's fixed stare. There had been something hard and calculating in it—enough to make her fingers falter into a discord. General laughter had followed fast upon it with the gentlemen remarking that her mind must have turned upon "Love in the village of Washington," whereupon Rayburn had struck an attitude and warbled another song from that operetta. It had concerned a hard-hearted wench named Dolly. Kitty blushed as she recalled the last verse:

> "Her swelling bosom, tempting ripe,
>   Of fruitful autumn was the type,
> But when my tender tale I told,
>   I found her heart was winter-cold."

Impossible not to notice that Rayburn's eyes had strayed to her bosom—fortunately well-covered by her modest muslin gown—but oh, how he had pronounced that "tempting ripe," rolling it around on his tongue! She had darted a speaking glance at her mother only to find her smiling and beating out the melody with her forefinger.

"Could she not see that they were flirting with me—the two of them? And must I be kind to them then?" she murmured resentfully.

"Beg pardon, Miz Kitty?" Little Becky Lou ceased her brushing.

"Nothing, Becky Lou, and you can go now." Kitty smiled at the child. She was pretty—pale cafe-au-lait colored skin and long-lashed black eyes. She also gave promise of being a very good maid; in fact, though only fourteen, she was already very skillful in arranging hair.

Evidently with that skill in mind, she said, "You sure you don' want me to stay an' plait your hair for the night, Miz Kitty?"

"No, Becky, that will be all."

"Yes'm, Miz Kitty." The girl bobbed a curtsey and slipped quietly from the chamber.

Kitty's hair felt warm about her shoulders, and for a moment she was sorry she had not let Becky Lou finish her work—but she *did* want to be alone. She moved toward her window and leaned out. It had grown cooler, but the air was still warm. It had been warm in the music room, too. She had been so glad when the evening had ended, but thinking on it, she still felt uneasy. She had no trouble attributing this sensation to the fact that Rayburn Abbott was in the house, his chamber being at the end of the hall. She wondered how long he would stay; no time period had been mentioned, but certainly, as caretaker of his brother's plantation, he could not remain indefinitely. She hoped he would take his departure very soon. It was odd how very much she disliked and feared him. She paused in her thinking—did she really fear him? He was rude, unmannerly, she did not care for the way he stared at her—but to be actively frightened of him? Generally she was not afraid of anyone. Perhaps it was the color of his eyes. . . . A breeze fanned her face and there was a rustling among the trees below in the garden. Staring down into the darkness, she found it illuminated in part by thousands of lightning bugs, tiny glowing morsels looking as if they might have been chipped from a star—a falling star which had crashed upon the earth and splintered all to pieces.

There were numerous superstitions about lightning bugs. Jael had told her that if one came into the house, a stranger might be expected, and that if two flew in, it meant a marriage.

"I'll have to go down and catch a pair of you," she whispered. "And then Robert will come riding back from Washington and . . ." She sighed, wishing once more that she had not paid any attention to Wellington Abbott and wondering how Julie was faring. Had she seen Robert? The idea did not appeal to Kitty. Julie was a flirt and . . . She tensed. Someone had knocked upon her door, a soft knock, more like a scratch, really. She did not like the sound of it; her mother did not knock that way, nor did any of the servants. She tiptoed across the floor and, coming close to the door, she reached for the key and was about to turn it when the door was pushed open and she found Rayburn Abbott on the threshold.

A step brought him inside to smile down at her. "Well," he drawled, "I'm glad you've not retired for the night yet, honey-sweet."

"What are you doing in my room?" Kitty demanded furiously, as she backed away from him. "Get out of here."

"Now is that any way to speak to your uncle, my pretty?" He moved toward her.

She was trembling, and to her extreme annoyance her voice shook as she answered, "You're nothing of mine and nothing to me."

"But I hope that's not a lasting condition," he returned softly. "You are very beautiful, little niece. I've been lonely in that big old chamber down the hall. This one's much more to my taste."

"If you don't get out, I shall scream."

"Scream away, my lovely," he laughed. "Your mama's taken her nightly laudanum and your step-papa's got an odd complaint. Come nightfall, he grows deaf. I don't expect he told you about that . . . but there's much you don't know about your family, though I doubt you'll be sayin' that tomorrow morning, pretty Kitty. I hear that's how you're known in these parts. Soooof—" His voice broke and to Kitty's astonishment, he started to fall but was caught from behind by Ben, one of the house servants, who, in addition to holding the sagging Rayburn's

20

collar in one hand, had a small wooden truncheon in his other hand. Smiling at Kitty, he flung the unconscious man over his shoulder and went quietly out of the room just as Jael hurried inside to put an arm around the shaken Kitty. She was followed by Becky Lou, who hastily closed and locked the door.

"Don' you say nothin'," Jael cautioned. "Jus' listen to what I got to say. You ain' got no time to lose. Ben's put Mr. Rayburn back in his room an' then he's goin' down to harness up the gig an' he'll drive you an' Becky Lou here to the river. He has a friend who'll ferry you across. Come dawn, you ought to be near Washington an' Ben's friend'll see you get to Mr. Robert. You can't stay here no more. Mr. Wellington an' his brother, they have it all fixed between 'em that Rayburn's goin' to bed you an' wed you for love an' money. They was a settlin' it between 'em at supper—didn't pay no mind to Oscar what was removin' the dishes—an' when Becky Lou come out of your room, she seen 'em wi' their heads together down the hall an' tol me an' I got Ben. Sorry you needed to be scared so, but we couldn't catch him afore he come to your room. Now don' you argue, child. You git."

"I will," Kitty added breathlessly. "But—but what about mama? What's she going to think? Will you tell her . . ."

"I won't tell her nothin'. You just write me a note for her sayin' as how you've gone to Mr. Robert . . . but don' say nothin' about Mr. Rayburn, because she wouldn' believe you an' I'll not have her upset any more'n she's goin' to be when she finds you high-tailed it outa here."

"Jael, won't Ben get into trouble, hitting Rayburn and taking the gig?"

"Bless you, child. Mr. Rayburn never knowed what hit him, an' he won't be able to complain about his sore head to nobody, neither, on account of all the questions'd be asked. An' Ben oughta be back afore dawn . . ."

In an amazingly short time, Becky Lou had packed a bandbox and followed Kitty down the back stairs through the kitchens and into the stableyard, where Ben was waiting with the gig.

"Oh, Jael!" Kitty turned to the woman who was standing beside her, looking more sphinx-like than ever. "I'll never be able to thank you enough." She threw her arms around the old woman.

"Don' thank me, Miz Kitty." Jael's voice was husky which was as close as she ever came to showing emotion. "I might be sendin' you right into the arms of the British."

"As I told you earlier today, Jael, better a Redcoat than Rayburn—but it won't be either." Kitty smiled ecstatically. "It will be Robert Heath!"

Two

"I will not go!" Mrs. Heath spoke decisively, as usual.

"Oh, my . . . oh, Miz Kitty," Becky Lou quavered.

Kitty, leaning from the front window of the Heaths' mansion on Y Street, had a view of coaches and wagons full of personal belongings and household goods rumbling down the dusty thoroughfares that must eventually bring them onto the Bladensburg Road and thence to comparative safety in nearby Georgetown. Modish gentlemen on horseback accompanied them and frantic ladies craned their necks from windows of the vehicles, their eyes wide and staring, almost as if they could see the approaching British armies.

Kitty watched them with a grim little smile. It was almost as if Jael's prophecy had come true. She had reached Washington the previous morning and if Robert's mother continued her stubborn refusal to leave until her son returned to escort her, they might very well be captured by the British. Yet, that, she decided with a shiver, was still preferable to the fate she had avoided at The Oaks.

She sighed. She had had only the briefest time with Robert. He had been bound out of Washington on a mission for Mr. Madison and was just about to leave when she had arrived. At first meeting, seeing his astonishment and disapproval at her coming such a long way with only her maid as a companion, she had been daunted. However, all that had changed once she had explained about Rayburn Abbott's invasion of her chamber. Then, of course, he had cosseted and comforted her, the while he had roundly cursed her would-be seducer and his brother, vowing he would slit both their gullets once he was back at Heathlands. She smiled, remembering the very satisfactory kiss he had given her. In fact, there had been several kisses and to think about them was to miss him more than ever. Yet she wished he had not entrusted her with the task of persuading his mother to leave Washington. "In case I don't get back in time, I'd like to know she was safe," he had told her worriedly.

"You oughtn't to come back at all," she had protested, "not if we're in such danger."

"I must—but I don't want mother or you to be here. You persuade her that she must go."

"I'll do my best," she had responded dubiously.

She had done just that but Mrs. Heath had turned a deaf ear to all her pleas and warnings. With the stubbornness so aptly described by Adeline, she had dug her heels in and balked, and Kitty did not see any way of getting her to change her mind.

Drawing back from the window because it was very

hot—even hotter than it had been at home and the roads shimmering like streams under that relentless sun —Kitty turned to face Mrs. Heath once more. The old woman stared back at her grimly, her lips compressed and, very likely, Kitty thought wearily, her teeth gritted. It was an expression she had seen reflected on Robert's face but more felicitously because he was so very handsome. He had looked wonderfully well the previous morning, neatly garbed in his dark suit, his Hessian boots polished to a high shine and his linen almost blindingly white. To think of him now was to get delicious shivers all over her body, but she could not think of him, only of her task. Figuratively girding her loins for another foray against the "enemy," she said, "Mrs. Madison is very likely on her way by now."

"I imagine *she* is," snapped Mrs. Heath in the tone she usually employed when discussing the President's wife. "Always was a namby-pamby. I've known Dolley Todd since she was knee-high to a grasshopper—always in a rush! Didn't wait until poor Mr. Todd was cold in his grave before she up and married Jemmy Madison. Disgraceful I called it then—disgraceful I call it now. And queening it over the lot of us from the President's mansion, if you please . . . shameful! Ought to be back in her mother's boarding house, setting out towels for her guests. That's—"

"Mrs. Heath," Kitty interrupted imploringly, "the British are coming."

Those words had scarcely left her lips when a distant but threatening rumble of cannon fire underlined them.

"Oh, my stars!" Becky Lou rolled her eyes and looked longingly in the direction of the door.

"The British, humph!" Mrs. Heath, tall, spare, white-haired and commanding of eye, as became the relict of General Andrew Ewing Heath of the Continental

Army, stared at Miss Maynard as if mentally decrying her lack of inches and slightness of build, while in turn Kitty reluctantly recalled her stepfather's words regarding Mrs. Heath's qualifications to be a general herself. "I," continued the lady, "am not going to be turned out of my home by a passel of Redcoats!" Marching across the room, she seized a musket from its place over the mantelpiece and thrust it toward Kitty. "You see this?" she intoned. "The General shouldered it during the whole of the Revolution. He could pick a Britisher off at fifty paces and I'll warrant I can do the same, from this very window! However, if you're so all-fired determined to leave, I shan't stop you—only I suspect you wouldn't want to go back to The Oaks. That Wellington Abbott—never could abide him. If you'd been his flesh and blood kin, I wouldn't have allowed Robert to become engaged to you—not on a bet, I wouldn't."

Kitty felt her hackles rise. Mrs. Heath had spoken as if Robert were a puppet to be worked by strings only she could pull. It was not true, she thought indignantly, he loved her as much as she loved him, and he would not let his mother influence him as to his choice of bride. Thinking of his request, she plunged once more into the fray. "Mrs. Heath, Robert expects us to be on our way to Georgetown. *Please*—"

"I am not leaving until he returns," snapped Mrs. Heath. Striding to the large Queen Anne chair which was her favorite seat—mainly, Kitty guessed, because it resembled a throne—she sat down and placed the musket across her knees. "From what I know about the British, rascals all though they may be, they do not make war on defenseless ladies. However, you mustn't pay me any mind, Kitty. I know you must be scared. You go onto Georgetown. Jake and Bill will guard you well."

26

"I am not scared—but it's half past three and Robert said we have to—"

"Make tracks!" Becky Lou burst out. "Ma'am," she turned her big eyes on Mrs. Heath, "we jus' can't stay here an' have them British eat us all up."

"Eat you all up!" Mrs. Heath chortled. "Bless you, child, they're not cannibals. Just low-down reprobates who haven't learned in thirty-eight years that we are no longer a possession of the British crown and subservient to his lunatic Majesty George the Third or his reprehensible son. But they will before this war is over. They are going to have their noses rubbed in defeat just like they did when General Washington chased them back to England. And it's a sight too bad he's cold in his grave. We haven't had his like since. Johnny Adams, Tom Jefferson, Jemmy Madison, t'isn't one of 'em could fit into his slippers, let alone his boots!"

As Mrs. Heath pontificated, Kitty stood and listened, while she felt her soul pacing back and forth across the room the way her stepfather did whenever he was nervous or upset. She could imagine he was doing plenty of pacing at this moment—and his brother as well. They must have been fit to be tied when they had found her gone, and she could imagine that Rayburn Abbott had a very bad headache. She hoped that they would not take it out on the servants—but, on second thought, they could not. Those who worked at The Oaks were there because they wanted to be: her father had freed his slaves years before he died. Her face softened . . . only a few of them had left. Most of them had stayed because Sam Maynard was so kind to them. Adeline, too, was kind as she had proved on that long-ago day when she had had her argument with Mrs. Heath. Her mother must have been the victor in that argument, but of course she had

27

not needed to persuade Mrs. Heath to her point of view. She could not have done it. Only Robert might have persuaded Mrs. Heath to change her mind—but of course, if he were here, she wouldn't have needed any persuading. Meanwhile, as everyone knew, the British were only a few miles away and would probably be in Washington by nightfall.

Though Kitty was *not* scared, she was filled with a sense of foreboding. She was not afraid of the British who were reputed to be polite and orderly, not harassing the citizenry, except for that portion of it which took up arms. Kitty frowned, wondering why she was so sure that something menacing was hanging over her head. It was not unlike the uneasiness that had possessed her two nights ago at The Oaks—but that had been caused by the sudden appearance of Rayburn Abbott. This present fear was more amorphous. However, possibly she could narrow it down to her present situation. . . . No, it was something else.

An old memory inserted itself into her consciousness. Years ago, there had been a slave called Fania on the plantation; she had had the reputation of being a conjure women able to see into the future. Coming upon little Kitty, who had been playing at the edge of the fields, she had stopped to stare at her out of huge, cloudy gray eyes, startingly light in her dark face. Seizing Kitty's hand, she had intoned, "I am told to tell you . . . this yo' future. Danger an' fire an' an ocean crossed . . . Trust not where you'd trust the most. You remember what I tol' you an' you be safe." She had released the child's hand and strode off without looking back.

That night Kitty had dreamed of her, seeing those huge eyes, grown even larger, boring into her and she had screamed aloud until her nurse had fetched her papa. Listening to the sobbed-out tale of her encounter with

Fania, he had only laughed, "African superstition, my love." And added, "The only sort of seeing into the future anyone can do is with a spyglass."

A spyglass! Kitty's eyes sparkled as she recalled that Robert owned one and that it might very likely be upstairs in his chamber. With a spyglass and standing up on the widow's walk, which Captain Fowler, who had built this house, had constructed, she could at least see into the distance and perhaps she might get a glimpse of scarlet in the woods that lay beyond the city. If she could sight such corroborating evidence of the approaching British, she would have a stronger argument to offer Mrs. Heath.

"Harrummph!" Mrs. Heath cleared her throat loudly.

Roused from her thoughts, Kitty found the old lady's bright eyes fixed on her. There was a gleam of suspicion in them. "You're mighty quiet, Kitty Maynard, and you look as if you're cogitating hard. What're you planning?"

Meeting that quizzical stare, Kitty flushed. "Nothing," she said airily.

"I thought you might be thinking up some more arguments," said the lady provocatively.

"No. That would be foolish. You have made up your mind."

"That I have," agreed the woman who would soon be Kitty's mother-in-law. But why did she have such difficulty in believing that? It was more than merely disliking her, it was another . . . could she liken it to Fania's prediction? No, she would not, but supposing Robert were in trouble or had met with a misadventure . . . ? She would not even think of it!

She said, "I thought I'd go upstairs and see if there's anything I have left behind. Robert could return at any moment and it occurs to me that I might have so done. I often do." A glance at Becky Lou told her that the girl was on the point of assuring her that she had not. Fixing a quelling eye upon her maid, she shook her head slightly, hoping the girl would interpret this sign correctly. She was relieved to see Becky Lou close her mouth. She smiled at Mrs. Heath. "I hope you'll excuse me."

"Gladly. You're sitting around here like a broody hen, only making me nervous. I tell you we've nothing to fear from the British."

"Very well, Mrs. Heath," Kitty allowed, and at her maid's rising she added, "You needn't come with me, Becky Lou."

She was up the long, steep staircase in minutes and into the shadowy expanse of Robert's chamber. She felt reluctant at invading this territory for if he had been there he would not have approved; but if he had been with them, she would not need to be trespassing! An odor smote her nostrils, making her flush—the cologne he used brought him as strongly to her mind as if he were standing beside her looking down at her out of his deep-set gray eyes. They were the legacy of his father, just as his nose and mouth were inherited from his mother. Fortunately, Kitty reflected, he did not resemble Mrs. Heath enough to depress her. She made a face. It was wrong of her to be so totally unenamored of the woman, particularly since she was doomed to be in her society for a long time, it being more than likely that even if Robert were to receive an assignment to the diplomatic staff of a foreign embassy, Mrs. Heath would accompany them.

Kitty ventured further into the room. There was his big four-poster and his highboy, both pieces sent up from Heathlands. On the wall between the windows was a mirror long enough to encompass his six-foot-two-inch frame. Stepping closer to it, she saw several white lengths of muslin lying on the floor, hinting at his valet's nervous fingers yesterday morning. Robert had become very demanding about his personal appearance, equally demanding when it came to hers. More than once he had complained that, while he could not quarrel with Becky Lou's hairdressing, he did not think the maid turned Kitty out in "slap-bang" style. He had scoffed when she protested that the maid was learning and had said masterfully, "When we're wed, you must have a personal maid with *experience*. Mother will choose one for you."

Mindful of this dire threat, Kitty regarded herself in the glass, critically inspecting her sprig muslin gown. In her rush to get away, Becky Lou had been able to pack only three changes of garments and she was pleased that the girl had remembered without being told that this was her very favorite. It was new and copied from a drawing in *La Belle Assemblée,* to which mama had subscribed until hostilities prevented its being sent from London.

The gown was very high in the waist and adorned with green ribbons that matched her eyes. There was a slight edging of lace around the neck, which was lower than she was wont to wear and had elicited raised eyebrows from Mrs. Heath; but it was cool and that was the reason Kitty had donned it.

Her glance rose from garments to face and wetting a finger, she smoothed her eyebrows. These, arched and dark, were the same color as the long eyelashes. She laughed ruefully. Mrs. Heath had disapproved of them, too, accusing her of painting them, but the finger that had smoothed them was bare of tell-tale smudges. She was, she thought, very pleased with features which everyone she knew agreed to be beautiful. Her hair was a different matter. Though he had never said as much, she feared Robert did not approve of it. It was too bright and curled too riotously around her vivid little face.

There had been a painful hiatus in their friendship

when he had gone to Harvard in far-away Massachusetts and for a short space of three months, his letters had been full of descriptions detailing the charms of a certain Patience Carew, whose shining bands of brown hair had proved to be particularly beguiling to Mr. Heath. Kitty had tried to smooth down her hair with pomade and broad ribbons but to no avail. Fortunately, when Robert came home, he had seemingly forgotten all about Miss Carew and her shining bands. Kitty stuck her tongue out at the image in the glass and whirled over to the highboy, which was also in disarray, with all his brushes lying out instead of being put into drawers—his valet having gone with his mother's maid to Heathlands. Picking up one of the brushes, Kitty saw strands of his chestnut-brown hair in it. She put the brush down.

"Oh, Robert, Robert, I wish you were here," she said wistfully. She hoped he would not blame her for failing to convince Mrs. Heath she should leave. Yet, she thought, frowning, he must know his mother better than she did—consequently, he could not be surprised at that failure. Possibly it would not *be* a failure if she were to sight the British. She was, she remembered, there for a purpose.

She did not find the spyglass on the top of the highboy or on his dresser. There was, of course, the possibility that his servant had taken it back to Heathlands—but it could also be in one of his drawers. She regarded them doubtfully, being sure he would not want her rummaging through them. Still, there was no help for it. Turning back to the highboy, she opened the first drawer. "Oh!" She clapped her hands in delight. The spyglass was there—right on top of a pile of cravats! Seizing it, she hurriedly left the chamber.

As she went up to the third floor, Kitty remembered Robert's tales of the house's builder and former owner.

Captain Fowler had been often observed striding back and forth on his roof, spyglass in hand, scanning the distant Potomac in much the same way he had once scanned the seas that had stretched before his Cape Cod dwelling. A veteran of the Revolutionary War, he had been respected but judged a harmless eccentric, particularly when he had warned of a British invasion by river, long after hostilities were at an end. She shivered. Here was more evidence that predictions could occasionally be accurate. Or had it been merely common sense? On approaching the stairs that led up to the Captain's aerie she saw that they were very dusty, giving the impression that no one had used them at any recent date.

That surprised her. If she had been Robert, she would have loved to view the city from this vantage point—and a few years ago, he, too, would have thought it a fine adventure. However, he had changed considerably from the boy she had known at home. Unbidden, Rayburn Abbott's mention of his pomposity flitted through her mind. Indignantly, she banished it. He was not pompous; he was just more dignified and that was only natural. After all he had a position to maintain. Still, if she had been Robert, she would have gone up on the roof to admire the view. She could imagine that it would be exciting to see most of Washington spread like a map below her. She hurried up the steps.

The door at the top opened outward. Judging from the difficulty she had trying to push it back, she was reasonably sure that it had not been opened since the death of Captain Fowler, ten years earlier. However, small and slim as she was, she had always possessed a wiry strength; and, after several attempts, she prevailed, realizing in that moment that some of her difficulties had been caused by the strong wind that buffeted her as she emerged, blowing her hair into her eyes and pressing her back against the railing of the widow's walk. As she stood there, trying to get her bearings, the door slammed behind her. She hoped that the sound had not been heard downstairs; it was quite possible that Mrs. Heath might mistake it for a shot, driving her to the windows, her musket primed for reprisals. She giggled at that image but sobered quickly. It would not be amusing if the old lady were to open fire on the invading Britsh. She was sure that the soldiers would not take kindly to snipers, even if they proved to be contumacious old women. However, by the time the British arrived, they would most likely be well on their way to Georgetown—for surely Robert would return soon!

Kitty lifted the spyglass to her eye and then had to take it down again. The wind was too strong for her to hold it steady, nor could she even stand there. She stepped over to one of the two chimneys, pressed against it, and raised the glass again. There was an unpleasant pounding in her throat. For argument's sake, she half-wanted to see the gleam of scarlet amidst the dusty close-growing trees upon that distant road; but actually, she did not want to see it at all, nor did she.

The woods at the edge of town were even denser than she had thought, but there were still departing carriages and wagons on the Bladensburg roadway and none were halting as they surely must if confronted by an approaching battalion. Half-disappointed, half-relieved, she moved around the chimney out of the sun and turned the glass in the direction of the President's mansion. It stood square and upright amidst its wide and barren expanse of grounds. There was, she thought, a depressing loneliness about it. Usually the front yard was crowded, but now it was empty. Indeed, no matter where she focused her glass, the streets were deserted and the few houses that fronted them looked similarly vacant though she knew that some of Washington's inhabitants had stubbornly insisted upon remaining in the town—or city; she mentally amended, recalling Robert gravely reproaching her for describing the nation's capital as a town.

"It is named Washington *City*," he had emphasized in that new instructing tone of voice he was beginning to employ whenever he spoke to her. "You must remember, dear Katherine, that it is also the *first* city in the country."

"Katherine." She laughed ruefully. Of late, he had taken to calling her that rather than Kitty, which, in his estimation lacked dignity. She had reminded him that the President's wife was named Dolley—but he had replied that no one who was a member of real Washington Society admired Mrs. Madison. "She does not have your breeding or background," he had explained loftily. "She is a very simple little woman—a nobody. Your father was a senator and both your parents have their roots deeply embedded in England's aristocracy, while my family can claim a similar heritage."

Kitty smiled derisively. Under the present circumstances, Robert had best remain silent about their British connections. As for herself, she had never been impressed by her lineage. She was proud and happy to be an American. Indeed, Robert's emphasis upon his Englishness bespoke a snobbery she could not admire. However, she reflected philosophically, though there were certain characteristics that she wished Robert had not possessed, one could not hope for perfection; the main thing was, he was attractive enough to please anyone and certainly he pleased her!

She lifted the spyglass to her eye again, fixing it on the intersecting streets that, from this height, looked like a geometrical drawing of triangles and parallelograms. There was Pennsylvania Avenue on which lay the President's Mansion and the Capitol and . . . She shuddered, envisioning the vast empty spaces between the streets and the swiftly flowing river filled with enemy soldiers. The threat of their imminent arrival was once more large in her consciousness. She ran a hand through her wind-tossed hair and found it wet with sweat. It was very warm on the roof—time to go down from the depressing spectacle of this soon-to-be-invaded city.

With some difficulty, she made her way back through the clawing winds to the door and grasped its handle. Uttering a cry of pain, she released it quickly. It was metal, and the sun had made it burning hot. She gathered a fold of her skirt, wound it around her hand and seized the handle again. To her surprise, the door did not immediately open. Kneeling, she wrapped both hands in the protecting material and pulled once more, but to no avail—it would not budge.

She regarded it with horror: evidently the wood was swollen from the heat, and if that were true, she could only wait until it cooled down—which would not happen until nightfall. She could not remain on the roof that long! Her momentary panic quickly subsided. She would not need to remain there. Undoubtedly Mrs. Heath or Becky Lou would miss her and come in search of her. When they did not find her, they must logically assume that she was on the roof—or would they? She had told them nothing of her plans. With a cold feeling in her breast, she recalled those dusty steps. No one in that household had ever penetrated to the roof. Yet, if she were to bang on the door and call, they, searching for her, must hear her and come to her aid; but how would she *know* when they were looking for her? She would need to pound and cry out at intervals; or possibly she could attract the attention of someone passing on the street below—except that there was no one about! She brightened. Robert would be arriving soon and she would be able to alert him!

A rueful little smile played about her mouth. She would surely receive a long lecture on her impulsiveness. It was a characteristic that Mr. Heath had long been wont to decry. She would be unable to produce an answering argument. It had been impulsive *and* extremely foolish of her to venture out on the roof without at least letting Becky Lou know what she had in mind. As Jael was fond of telling her, "Hindsight'll never take the place of foresight, Miz Kitty."

However, it was useless to cry over spilt milk. Kitty settled down in the shadow of the chimney to wait until a time, when, according to her calculations, those below must become anxious about her failure to return to them. And ... there was always, she reminded herself—albeit not very hopefully—an outside chance that they might guess where she had gone.

* * *

The acrid smell of burning wood, an ominously bright glow at the end of one street, the sounds of sharply-barked commands, of marching feet, of an amalgam of voices echoing through the night, reached Kitty. Crouched at the railing, she stared fearfully down into the darkness. The British had come and had been greeted by volleys of shots in the vicinity of that blaze. She guessed that the razing of the house was a retaliatory measure, for there had been no similar fires as yet.

"Robert, Robert, Robert," she murmured distractedly, wondering what had happened to him. She stroked her scraped and bleeding knuckles with her smarting palm. She was tempted to try the door again—but her throat was sore from crying for aid. Time and time again during the last few hours, she had crawled back to it, to beat upon its surface, to tug at its unyielding handle—all to no avail. No one had had the imagination to search for her; or if they had, they had come at a time when she was resting, exhausted.

Staring into the darkness, she blinked away frightened tears. "If I had but considered . . . but I could not have known the door would slam! Still, I should have told them I was coming up here . . . and Robert, where is he? Why hasn't he returned?" She had been asking herself that question all the time she had been stranded on the roof—but the answers which came to her now were no longer centered upon unavoidable delays. Something terrible must have happened to him! Perhaps he had fallen into an ambush and lay dead! Perhaps he had run afoul of the British and had been taken prisoner. Perhaps . . .

Frantically, she ran her hands through her tangled hair; she must not, could not, *dared not* search for reasons. It was futile, and she could drive herself to distraction. She must think of a way to get down—but that was futile, too. Then she gasped, for to her left the sky was glowing orange again—other fires were being kindled, and suddenly the darkened windows of the President's Mansion were agleam, shining as brightly as they did on nights when Mrs. Madison held her famous levees. But, Kitty realized with a shudder, it was more than candleglow that was illuminating them—a thousand, million candles could not have produced so brilliant a light!

She rose and backed against the nearest chimney and clutched the cooling brick as she watched in horror while flames curled around windows and shot forth from doors and vivid sparks were wind-swirled above the burning building. Fury dried her tears. The British ogres were destroying the seat of the Presidency! Her anger and horror increased as she saw flames leaping about the one finished wing of the Capitol. The smell of smoke was being borne toward her on the rising wind. She sank to her knees, grasping the rail and shuddering: her horror at the wanton destruction had narrowed into fear for herself. There was every chance that sparks from the monstrous conflagration could reach this house, invade its windows, and set it ablaze as well. She would be burned to death in her unwittingly-chosen trap!

Her despair lasted only a moment. She jumped up and whispered defiantly, "I shan't die. I'm not ready. Not at all. I've but turned eighteen and that's not nearly long enough to live. I must think of something!"

She tensed. She heard voices; judging by the sound of them, they were directly below her on the street. Soldiers! She could call to them. They were British, but that did not matter—better capture than death by burning! She dashed toward the railing, then paused, alerted by the crack of gunfire at very close range. It was followed almost immediately by a hoarse cry, which, in turn, was succeeded by an eldritch shriek: "Back, back, ye varmints, or I'll blow your blasted heads off!" Mrs. Heath was making good her earlier threats.

Kitty, clenching jaw and fingers, shook her head, mentally cursing the woman for her abysmal stupidity, as she heard a whole volley of answering shots issuing, she guessed, from some half-dozen muskets. Feet pounded across the street; there was loud pounding on the front door and a noise as if it had been wrenched back and slammed against the wall.

Another shriek resounded in Kitty's ears. "Damn ye, ye Redcoat swine, ye villains, ye—" Mrs. Heath's cries were abruptly muffled as if someone had put a hand over her mouth.

"The house—the house—burn the house," barked a

young but authoritative voice and the darkness below was brightened by a blazing torch.

Possessed by an almost mindless frenzy, Kitty clambered over the railing and slid down the steep, slanting roof to a projecting ledge that ran below a pair of dormer windows. She peered over the ledge, and came to face a little group of soldiers standing in the street.

"Hear me," she screamed loudly. "Help me, *pleeeease!*"

Pulses pounding, throat aching, heart thumping, she prayed to God and all his angels to direct the soldiers' glances toward her, but to no avail. They went on talking among themselves and gesticulating at the house with—horror of all horrors—the torch. They had not heard her; naturally they could not hear her voice amidst all the noise and confusion that echoed from every city street. She would surely die—no she would not, not if she could possibly help it!

She eased her foot out of her little morocco slipper and reached for it, but it slid away too quickly and fell off the roof into the foliage, unperceived by the men below. Slowly, carefully, she wriggled her other foot out of her slipper, pinioned it with her toe and, with one hand, managed to grasp it. Twisting about, she clutched the window ledge and threw her shoe. She saw it strike one man's shoulder, saw him stare down at it as it fell at his feet—wondering, the dolt, from whence it had come?

"Please look up, please, God, let him look up!" she prayed again. He was turning. He was glancing upward—but how might he see her in the darkness? The only reason she could see him was because of the light from the torches.

"*Heeeellp!*" she screamed again, the effort tearing her throat. Had he heard? Did he understand that he must secure a torch? It seemed he did for a second later he, or someone else held up a torch and moved toward the house. She blinked against the brightness of the flames held up just below her and saw that two other men had joined the torch bearer. *"Help me!"* She had to force the sound out of a throat that felt as if it were closing.

The soldiers stared at each other and another man joined them; there was the gleam of gold in the firelight. It was on his shoulders—epaulettes; he must be an officer. Lifting a torch, he looked up at her and yelled something but she could not hear him amid the clamor. She shook her head and pointed at the railing, wondering if he understood that that was the way she had come. Then she gasped, for she felt herself slipping. She clutched at the window ledge and held onto it tightly, while he said something to the soldiers with him. In another moment, two of them had disappeared from her view, going in the direction of the house.

She dared exhale a sigh of relief, but it died aborning. Rescue might be on its way, but how would they know where to search? The officer was still below, but he was no longer looking in her direction. He was talking to the other men; they were moving up and off and it seemed as if he meant to go with them. She opened her mouth to scream again but no sound emerged. Her voice was gone! Hopelessly, she leaned her head against the window ledge. Her arms were getting tired. She wished she dared climb back to the widow's walk, but that was too dangerous. She must remain where she was, though how long she could continue to hold onto the ledge she did not know. But she would not give up hope, not yet. There was a possibility they had seen the railing and understood its significance. That would explain why she was on the roof . . . but suppose they had not seen it?

A nearby smashing of glass almost caused her to lose her precarious grip—then she was aware of light flickering through the window panes and, looking around, found that the soldiers had had the good sense to come into the attic. More glass was breaking, falling to the roof from the window opposite to the one she was clutching.

A soldier leaned out, sighted her and called, "Stay back, miss, an' we'll smash t'other window. D'ye understand?"

Unable to answer, she nodded several times and waited. In another moment, the window beside her had been similarly broken and one of the soldiers was framed in its aperture. He reached out his hand. "Easy, easy," he muttered. "Don't ye be afraid, little miss."

Edging closer to him, she felt herself seized about the waist. For a moment, she was panic-stricken, feeling her feet sliding out from under her—swinging wildly. Then, she was being held firmly and helped inside. Until that moment, Kitty had never been pleased by her slightness of figure and her lack of inches, but until that moment, she had never been dragged through a dormer window.

Set down, she found herself in a surprisingly cluttered attic. All about her were bits and pieces of furniture, discarded statuary, piles of unframed canvases and even a battered chaise-longue which, due to the lack of a leg, lay at a crazy angle; but it was here her soldier led her and she was glad enough to sink down upon it. Her legs, she had just discovered, had turned nerveless and were quite unable to support her. She smiled gratefully at her rescuers. In the flickering light from the candles they were holding, she found they looked alike enough to be brothers. It was not only their similar uniforms—both were medium-sized, blond, blue-eyed with sunburnt complexions, thick, sturdy bodies and big, broad hands, suggesting that before being called to the colors they might have been farmers.

As she reached this conclusion, she found they were staring at her and evidently forming conclusions of their own. They were also laughing immoderately. Catching a whiff of their breaths, she guessed the reason for that. They were both more than a little foxed—but that did not matter. All that mattered was that her terrifying ordeal was finally at an end. She wanted to thank them, but when she tried to speak all that emerged was a whisper. She smiled and pointed to her throat.

They exchanged glances. "Lost yer pipes, eh?" one of them said in a thick, almost unintelligible dialect. "T'was all that yellin', I'll be bound, eh, little lass?"

She nodded.

"Was ye long atop that there roof?" the other demanded.

Kitty nodded again and he continued, "Oi'd like to know wot you was a-doin' up on yon roof, but Oi'd guess ye'll not be able to tell a man."

As she smiled and shook her head, the first soldier said, "No, Jemmy, the poor little lass 'as lost 'er tongue."

"Aye, to be sure," Jemmy observed. "Only can't say as Oi don't like it better when a female don't speak." He winked at his companion. "Wot d'ye say, Dick?"

"Oi'd say it's much better," Dick agreed solemnly. "Most o' 'em got a sight too much to say for themselves. She be a pretty bit o'muslin, bain't she?"

"Damned pretty an' wi' that 'air, red an' a bit o' yeller in it, too. Always was partial to red 'eads. 'Ow 'bout you?"

"Oi ain't selective, red, yellow, black, brown. Long as t'ain't white like that old cat's as winged poor Charlie, but like you say, 'er color o' 'air ain't 'alf bad."

Listening to this peculiar exchange, Kitty was suddenly on her guard. There was something frightening in the way their bright eyes were roving over her face and body. She was unwillingly reminded of Rayburn Abbott's hard stare, and Wellington Abbott came to her mind, too. For the first time, she noticed that her gown was ripped in several places, one of them being at the shoulder, another at the knee, exposing a shift blackened by contact with the dusty roof. She tried to arrange her skirts to hide these rents and found her hands were trembling.

"Oi thought she were a sweet armful, the minute Oi seen 'er," Jemmy remarked.

"Oi thought so, too," Dick returned. "Only got to remember we got orders, 'ands off or old Cocky'll 'ave our 'eads."

"Aye, but 'e ain't 'ere an' nobody could 'ear nothink, if she was to cry out an' she oughtn't to cry out. Ought to be grateful, weren't for us, she might still be on that there roof."

"Might've fallen off by now, weren't for you'n me." Dick grinned. "An that 'd've been a fair waste."

"Aye, an 'ell of a waste." Jemmy sat down close to Kitty and swore softly as the chaise-longue tilted sharply under his weight.

"No good, that." Dick stared at it critically. He held up his candle and peered around the attic. Stepping into the shadows, he stumbled, cursed, then said gleefully, " 'Ere, look wot Oi've found."

"Wot?" Jemmy rose.

"Over 'ere. Cushions a bit dusty, but that don't matter, they be soft."

His back was to her and the other man out of sight. In the uncertain light of the candles they had set down on an adjacent table, Kitty saw a small door. She slipped off the chaise longue and made a dash for it, only to trip over what seemed to be a heap of carpets or a pillow. She fell sprawling.

" 'Ere!" Jemmy grabbed her. "Lass, lass!" He shook his head. "Where's yer gratitude?"

She tried to pull away from a hard grip on her waist but it only tightened, and her captor bent down suddenly and pressed a long kiss on her lips. A scream rose in her throat but emerged only as a tiny whimper, stifled by the sickening pressure of his wet mouth and, to her utter horror, his seeking tongue.

" 'Ere," growled Dick, "put 'er over 'ere an' share an' share aloike, Oi say."

Struggling, sobbing, her fists flailing impotently against Jemmy's scarlet coat, Kitty felt herself lifted and in seconds, she was thrust back against a heap of cushions. The two young men were kneeling on either side of her; their fingers fumbled at their belts. Moaning and trying to writhe away from them, she was reminded of something Mrs. Heath had once said regarding the "horrors of war," explaining that during the Revolution, many women had been "dishonored" by the invading Hessians. Asked what being "dishonored" entailed, Mrs. Heath had actually flushed and said brusquely that it had to do with a loss of innocence. With a horrid certainty, Kitty knew that she was about to suffer that loss. Their hot sweaty hands were traveling up her body. She cringed away from them. Scream after scream arose in her lacerated throat, emerging only as hissing sighs while their drunken laughter reverberated through the small room.

A sudden crash startled her and, from where she was lying, Kitty could see that the attic door had been thrown open. Her two assailants stiffened as a furious voice yelled, "What is the meaning of this!?"

The soldiers stumbled hastily to their feet. Dimly, Kitty saw that they were trying to straighten their clothing and, at the same time, stand at attention, at least as much

45

at attention as that sloping roof would allow. Both were speaking or, rather, mumbling in unison, and the other man, whoever he was, cut across their faltering words as he rasped brusquely, "Get out!"

They lost no time in obeying the order; and, shortly after they had scuttled through the low doors, she heard cries accompanied by loud thumping sounds, suggesting that in their hasty retreat, the pair had fallen down the stairs.

Kitty pulled together her disordered clothing and tried to rise but failed, finding that she was trembling all over. She blinked as a candle was held above her face. Her rescuer, his own features in darkness, said in slightly slurred tones, "I hope they didn't hurt you." He moved closer and looked down at her concernedly. She saw the gleam of gold epaulettes in the flickering flame, and realized that he was an officer, possibly the same officer she had seen in the street below. "Did they . . . are you hurt?" he asked, kneeling beside her. His breath also smelled of spirits but his voice was gentle, his manner courteous.

She shook her head. "N-no," she mouthed, then, with a second shake of her head, she burst into tears.

He quickly set the candle down on the table that held the other two and put his arms around her. He held her against him, saying comfortingly, "There, there, mustn't weep, poor mite. Jus' been such a night. . . . Ross's horse, mine, too, poor beasts, shot out from under us. And the flames, didn't like the flames, didn't mean to burn so much, but drank too much, wine and brandy . . . President's cellar, y'understan'. Bottles and bottles and bottles, full bottles and all of us so weary, marched all day. Blistering heat, never felt such heat. Marched all day, all day, men afraid, all of us afraid. . . . Shooting at us from treetops, couldn't see guns. Lost man in the swamp,

46

couldn't reach him . . . so many men, comrades, been with them long time . . . and so hot and smell of death . . . everywhere death. . . ."

These, too, were the horrors of war—infinitely more horrible than anything she might have suffered. Hearing his spent, weary voice, she forgot he was the enemy, forgot everything save that the man who had rescued her was racked with a pain she wanted to alleviate. Yet she had no comforting words to give him—she could not stop weeping, though whether she was crying for herself or because of what he had just told her, she did not know.

"Poor child, poor child." He stroked her hair gently. Then his hand fell on her bare shoulder. "So soft," he muttered. "Skin so soft . . ." He put his finger under her chin, and tilted her face toward the candle flame. "Lovely girl, so lovely." He ran his finger under her eyes. "Tears, muss not cry. Do not like to see you cry."

She sniffed and sniffed again but the gentleness with which he had spoken only brought more tears, and, not wanting him to see them, she buried her head amid the cushions. He put his arm around her. His grasp was tight, as tight as that of Jemmy, but she was not afraid. She had seen his face, haloed by a mist of tears and, though she would have been hard put to describe them, she had found his features to her liking; it seemed to her that warmth and kindness radiated from him. Her wild weeping turned into dry, hiccoughing sobs.

"There, there, poor little one," he murmured, patting her shoulder. He stretched out on the cushions beside her and pulled her against him so that her head lay near his heart—she could hear its steady beat beneath her ear.

She did not push him away. After her head-long flight from The Oaks, her wearisome arguments with Mrs. Heath, her painful sojourn on the roof and her recent terror, she felt as if she had found a haven—as if, indeed, her father's arms were around her. She had missed him so dreadfully. As she moved closer to the man beside her, she felt very tired, yet something told her she ought not to sleep. Then she heard the sound of his breathing; it was very even, very deep—he had fallen asleep! She knew she ought to free herself from his clutch—but she did not want to awaken him. In common with herself, he had suffered pain and loss and terror and . . . In the middle of this thought, her weighted eyelids dropped and she, too, fell fast asleep.

Three

The wind that had been blowing through most of the night had increased and a gust of it, heavily laden with smoke, came through the broken windows of the attic, awakening Kitty. She blinked away the blur of sleep, staring at the sloping walls bathed now in the gray light of early dawn.

For a moment, seeing the roof above her and the bits and pieces of furniture lying helter-skelter on the floor, she felt as if she might still be asleep and dreaming. The sound of a deep sigh and a spate of mumbled words brought a host of memories crowding into her mind. Suppressing a gasp, she turned to gaze down at the man in the creased and smudged red coat who lay beside her, his dark, tousled head buried in his folded arms. Hastily she edged away from him, her cheeks burning as she remembered that she had gone to sleep in his embrace—a man she did not know, had never seen before that night—whose features she could not even visualize, having viewed them only in the uncertain light of the candle he had been holding. She could recall only that he had been comforting and kind. He had seemed distressed over her woe and had soothed her fears. She had felt extraordinarily safe with him—but yet, he was a British soldier, one of those who had set fire to the President's Mansion!

She glanced about her and saw the small door through which he had come, through which *they* had come to rescue her, those two soldiers who might have exacted such a heavy price for their good deed. More memories tumbled back into her head and by turns she was hot and cold with embarrassment and fear. Then there was only fear, for Robert was back in her mind. She shuddered—what had happened to him? Had he returned? Had he come back to this house and been captured by the invaders?

"Oh, God," she whispered, "don't let anything happen to Robert or—" She experienced a certain reluctance as she added—"his mother."

Anger surged through her. Everything bad she had ever heard about Evadne Heath was true! She was stubborn, selfish, uncaring, unthinking, a tyrant! If it had not been for her refusal to leave without her son, even though she was well aware that she was endangering all of them through her mulish and ill-advised determination, they could have been safe in Georgetown! What could have happened to the old woman after that most injudicious attack on the enemy?

The enemy? It was amazing. Yesterday the word had meant very little to her. Today it had a whole spectrum of meanings: fire, death, invasion of a city, of a nation's capital and, more specifically, more painfully—

invasion of a body, a body which might have suffered. She was not sure *what* would have happened if the man at her side had not come; but he *had* come, he had saved her from those two men. She shuddered again. Yet it was selfish to think about that when so many frightful events had taken place. . . . But no, she could not concentrate on generalities, not yet.

She glanced down at herself and blushed to her toes for her gown was in appalling condition. Not only was it ripped at shoulder and knee, it was filthy from contact with that dusty, sooty roof and there was a dark stain on her skirt—a red blotch which looked like blood. Blood? Where might that have come from? Had she suffered a scratch and was unaware of it? She looked down and saw the officer had a bandage wrapped around his knuckles—a blood-stained bandage. He must have been hurt and when he had held her in his arms . . . Some memory of his fragmented speech came back to her. His horse had been shot from under him. That had distressed him, not for himself but for the animal. Her heart warmed toward him. He was kind; he had been kind to her, too. But she had not expected kindness from the British. She had not even thought of them as individuals. For the last two years, they had only been the Enemy—a faceless, menacing mass. But they had faces and one had not been menacing, at least not to her. She longed to thank him, but she did not want to awaken him, and she did want to be clean. There was a well in the back yard and her bandbox was in the drawing room with a change of clothing.

She glanced toward the door—how to reach it quickly without rousing him? She stared down at him again: his hair was darker than Robert's, blue-black and wavy. His eyes, she recalled, could also have been dark, but she was not sure of that. Probably she would not know him again if she were to meet him on the street. He had been only a presence in the night, a young man who had been kind. She flushed again, recalling how she had wept and how tender he had been, how gentle, how apologetic. To think on that was to be filled with a strange confusion which she did not understand, which she did not *want* to understand, which she must and would put out of her mind—immediately! She must leave the attic, but quietly.

It was growing lighter. A glance at the window showed her that the grayness had given way to pale blue, rose-tinged in the distances. It would be easier for her to make her way across that cluttered floor. Carefully, she edged away from him, thankful that he did not stir. She arose: she was very stiff, and her shoes, what had happened to them? Oh, yes, she had dropped them from the roof to alert the soldiers. She winced, not wanting to think of Dick and Jemmy. In her bandbox, there was another pair of slippers, unless the soldiers had appropriated it. Again she wondered what had happened to Mrs. Heath and to Becky Lou, poor child. If only the old woman had not fired on the soldiers! There was no use dwelling on that. She had fired, and fretting over her folly would not change matters in the least.

Kitty moved quietly, carefully across the room, managing to skirt the fallen furniture. Then her foot struck some object that went spinning across the floor. She froze, glancing back over her shoulder at her companion of the night. Much to her relief, he did not stir. Finally she reached the door. It was half open; when she slipped through it, she discovered that the stairs were only a few feet away.

Creeping down the steps, Kitty found all silent on the second floor. A look at the room she had occupied the night before last showed her that it was just as she left it: on the washstand was an ewer and a basin. She examined them hopefully but remembered that she had told Becky Lou to be sure to throw their contents out; even slightly dirty water would have done for a rough wash. She sighed and went on down the stairs. As she reached the front hall, there was an abrupt movement— a tall young soldier in a worn red coat came from a side door to confront her. He regarded her with surprise. " 'Ere," he grunted, "where'd you come from?"

She felt herself growing weak all over. In appearance he was much akin to her "rescuers." "I—I was upstairs," she explained and found that, though her voice had come back, it was very hoarse, a mere thread of breathy sound.

"Upstairs, eh?" To her consternation, a knowing smile lighted his eyes and he licked his lips. "You're the little wench wot were wi' the Major, eh? An' where d'ye think yer goin' now, lovey?"

Resentment at his insolence would have found expression in a hot answer had not Kitty remembered that she was his prisoner. She said, "I wanted to fetch fresh water for washing—there's a well out back."

"You better wait until 'e comes down," he replied. Jerking a thumb at the drawing room door, he added, "Get in there."

"But may I not—" she began.

"Get in there," he ordered roughly, "wi' the rest o' 'em."

Kitty paled. Mrs. Heath and Becky Lou must be being held prisoner in there. She did not want the old woman to see her so disheveled. "Please . . ."

"Go on, *get* in," he commanded, gesturing with his rifle.

Reluctantly, she opened the door. As she stepped over the threshold, a chair scraped back. "Kitty!"

"Robert!" She stopped dead, staring incredulously at the tall young man, who had just gasped out her name.

Relief and shock were mingled as she faced him. Her fears had been realized—evidently he had sustained rough treatment at the hands of the enemy soldiers. His right eye was swollen shut; his nose flattened and his lip split. The elegant coat he had worn yesterday morning was gone, his shirt was in rags. "Oh, Robert," Kitty sobbed. "Oh, my dearest, what has happened to you!"

"I—" he began only to be silenced by his mother's chill comment.

"Well, we didn't think we'd see you again!"

Spinning around, Kitty found Mrs. Heath sitting in her Queen Anne chair. She was pale but her deep-set eyes were full of anger. "What made you come back?" she demanded contemptuously.

"Come . . . back?" Kitty repeated confusedly.

"Yes." Robert's voice was edged with disapproval if not contempt. "Where did you go?"

"Go?" Her confusion deepened. "What do you mean?"

In a pained voice, Robert began: "Mother seems to believe that—"

"That you turned tail and ran away," accused Mrs. Heath. "What happened? They must've caught you and brought you back."

Indignantly, Kitty glared at her. "I was not 'brought back' as you are pleased to put it." She looked at Robert. "Is that what she's been telling you? I am supposed to have run away?"

"Yes. I must say that I was extremely disappointed—"

"You were disappointed!" she cried. "You . . . you actually *believed* that I had done such a thing when you'd entrusted me with the care of your mother? I wanted to leave for Georgetown. I begged her to go, but she'd not budge! Nothing I could say would persuade her to leave until you returned. Consequently, I went upstairs, on the roof to the widow's walk. I took your spyglass with me. I—I thought if the enemy proved to be on its way, I might tell her I had seen the British and then I'd be able to persuade her to do as you asked. Then, when I came out on the roof, the wind blew the door shut and it stuck. I couldn't get it open—I tried for hours and *hours,* but to no avail could I get back into the house. That is what happened. I wouldn't run! I am *not* a coward."

"You've been on the roof all this time?" he demanded.

His question brought back the unwelcome memory of her rescuers. She looked down. "Not all this time, but through yesterday afternoon and into the evening."

"She's lying," the old woman snapped. "Every word she's uttered's been a lie."

Kitty hands clenched into fists. "It's *not* a lie," she retorted. "I was on the roof when I heard you fire through the window." She stamped her foot. "How could you do anything so foolhardy? They were ready to burn the house down!"

Mrs. Heath's eyes gleamed. "Winged one of 'em," she said with considerable satisfaction. "Paid 'em back for what they done to that girl of yours."

"Becky Lou!" Kitty gasped. "They ... didn't hurt her?"

"Killed her dead as a doornail. Got her right between the eyes, a shot that was meant for me, no doubt."

"Oh, oh, *oh,*" Kitty gasped in horror. "Oh, God, poor Becky Lou—what'll her mother say?" Furiously, she cried, "If you hadn't shot at them ... it was all your fault!"

"Fool wench was at the window." Mrs. Heath shrugged. "Didn't have the sense she was born with."

"How can you be so unfeeling!" Kitty gasped. "She

was only fourteen and . . . oh dear." She could not restrain her sobs.

"Lord save us! One'd think she'd lost her last friend. There are plenty more where she came from, my girl."

"How dare you!" Anger replaced Kitty's grief. "She was my friend . . . she—"

"Just like your mother, you are. Soft, where you ought to take a whip to their hides."

"Mother," Robert spoke reprovingly, "you didn't tell me you'd shot at the soldiers. You should not have done that. It was most unwise."

"What else could I do?" she countered. "I was alone in the house and your fine fiancée hiding on the roof . . ."

"I was not hiding," Kitty contradicted. "I was trying to see if the British were coming."

"Lies," Mrs. Heath repeated loudly. "I was willing to leave. We were waiting on your return. Left us sitting here without a by-your-leave. It's your fault your girl was killed." She pointed an accusing finger at Kitty. "I always told you she didn't have gumption! High-tailed it out of here like a scared rabbit, that's what she did. She can talk all she likes but actions speak louder than words—that's what I say!"

Kitty blanched. For the moment she was stricken silent by the woman's outrageous falsehoods. Why was she lying? In that instant, she knew why. Mrs. Heath was attempting to remove the onus from her own ill-advised actions by heaping this calumny upon her head. Would Robert believe her? He had already believed her once, had actually thought she had deserted the old woman and with poor Becky Lou gone, there was no one to bear witness against Mrs. Heath—no one save herself to tell him the truth. Desperately, she turned toward him, then blinked against the light of the rising sun through the uncurtained windows. "Robert," she began. "You surely know me better than . . ."

"Kitty!" he interrupted loudly, his one good eye wide with shock. "What has happened to your gown—there's blood on it!"

"Blood?" Mrs. Heath echoed. Rising, she strode to Kitty's side and stared at her intently. "Good God, I believe she's been ravished."

"Ravished!" Robert repeated in horror.

"No," Kitty cried, "it's not *my* blood! The man who rescued me from—"

"And look at her gown!" Mrs. Heath continued inexorably. "Ripped at the shoulder, ripped at the thigh . . ."

"Oh, my God!" Robert exclaimed.

"Robert, nothing happened to me. The soldiers t-tried but *he* came and . . . and . . ."

"She's been ruined!" Mrs. Heath cried and to Kitty's horror, there was a triumphant note in her voice.

"Robert! It's not true. I swear it's not true. He only—"

"He? Who is he and what did he 'only' do to you? Look at her, Robert!"

The door was suddenly thrust open. " 'Ere be the wench wot were wi' you last night, Major." Kitty recognized the voice of the soldier she had seen in the hall and then another soldier strode into the room. Though he had the insignia of a major, he looked very young, not more than twenty-three or -four. He was tall and dark but the eyes he turned on her were a vivid blue.

"Ah, here you are, child," he began and hesitated, glancing at the other two occupants of the room.

"Yes, here she is," the old woman crowed. "Your victim!"

Tears stood in Kitty's eyes. She ran to him. "Tell them it's not true . . . tell them that you didn't touch me last night. Tell them we only—"

She was interrupted by Mrs. Heath's derisive laughter. "Yes, *tell* us how she came by that blood down her dress! Tell us she's not ravished and ruined. Tell us you didn't use her like your whore."

"It's not true!" Kitty stamped her foot. "It's not true!" She turned on the silent Robert. "You—you can't believe her," she faltered, looking into his shocked face.

He stared at her in horror. "There *is* blood on your dress and that soldier said he . . . you were with him last night. How can I believe . . ."

"How can you believe that nothing happened to her last night? How can you believe that she is speaking the truth? How can you believe that I did not take advantage of her last night? How can you believe that it is *my* blood you see upon her dress?" The Major held up his bandaged knuckle. He had paled and his blue eyes were very hard. Striding to Robert's side, he continued icily, "How can you believe this girl a liar? She has told you only the truth!"

"The truth?" Mrs. Heath's mocking laughter resounded through the room. "Here's gallantry, indeed. Marry your fiancée, my son. Take her to your bed and nine months from now when she drops her British bastard, claim it as your own."

"Mother!" Robert exclaimed.

"Madame." The Major turned on Mrs. Heath. "If you were a man, I'd thrust those words down your gullet with my fist." He stared at Robert. "Have you nothing more for your mother than this mild protest, no word of reproof? And have you no word of comfort for this poor child, whom I seem to have compromised? What manner of man are you to remain silent at such a time?"

"T'was her own folly," Mrs. Heath cried. "Your father, the Senator, would have been proud of his daughter, I have no doubt!"

Kitty had lost all desire to weep. "My father would have believed me when I told him I spoke the truth—no matter how much appearances and circumstances were against me."

"And still you have nothing to say, Master Robert?" the Major demanded.

"You have the advantage of me, Sir," Robert returned. "I do not know your name . . ."

"My name, Sir, is Quentin, but this you *do* know. You know that I have compromised this poor girl and that I may have ravished her—yet you do not step forward to avenge that wrong—you do not challenge me to a duel."

"I—" Robert began.

"Do not answer him, Robert. Can you not see that he is goading you?" shrilled Mrs. Heath.

"I have nothing else to say, Mother," Robert told her coldly. "It is beneath my dignity to speak with him. Nor am I in any position to challenge him, being, in effect, his prisoner!"

"And what do you say to this, Master Robert?" Moving closer to him, the Major struck him sharply across the cheek. "I release you from custody. You are no longer a prisoner. Name your time, name your weapon. Will it be swords or pistols? Yours is the choice."

As Kitty held her breath in amazement, Mrs. Heath screamed, "Neither! You'll not fight for the sake of this stupid little fool who deliberately placed herself in jeopardy!"

"Mother!" Robert's face was red and he was trembling. "I—I will not fight you, Sir, because I—am a m-man of peace and I—I . . ."

"Robert!" Kitty exclaimed. "I pray you'll say no more. Oh, God, you—you make me ashamed for you!" To her horror, her voice broke and she found herself weeping again.

Major Quentin put an arm around her shoulders. "Do not grieve, my dear," he said. "I do not know how you came to be in company with this pair—indeed, it passes all understanding—but you must not be afraid. Since the fault for what has occurred is mine. I shall try and make amends."

"Amends?" Mrs. Heath sneered. "What will you do, Major Quentin—restore her maidenhead?"

"Madame—" Major Quentin turned on her again. "Since by shape and feature, one must regard you as a female, I must refrain from dealing with you as you so rightly deserve—but since we British do not make war on women, I am forced to abide by our rules. However, neither of us need remain to suffer these slanders. Come, my dear."

Before Kitty quite knew what he was about, he had escorted her from the room. "We must talk," he began urgently. Then, directing a glance toward the young soldier by the door, he added, "You have my leave to stand outside, Corporal Hardy."

"Yes, Sir." Saluting smartly, the Corporal, his face now impassive, turned and marched outside, closing the door behind him.

"Come." Major Quentin led Kitty to a settle placed in the curve of the staircase. "We've little time and much to discuss. Please sit down."

Wonderingly, she obeyed. "I . . ." she began as the Major settled into the place beside her. She hesitated, realizing that she was not sure what she wanted to say. A thousand thoughts seemed massed in her head—Mrs. Heath's lies, Robert's doubts, his craven refusal to defend her, Major Quentin's quixotic intervention. It was all wrong. *Robert* should have been at her side, comforting her, not the man who had unwittingly stripped her of her honor. It should have been her fiancé, too, who was regarding her so earnestly, so pityingly.

"How did you come to be in company with such people?" he demanded.

"I have known Robert all my life. His father's lands march with The Oaks, my father's estate. We're both from Fairfax County—that's in Virginia. His mother has never liked me, but I thought that he . . . I believed . . ." A sob escaped her.

"Do not weep," he begged. "He's not worth one of your tears. You're well out of such a *mésalliance*. You may not agree with me as yet, but—"

"I *do* agree," she corrected. She brushed an impatient hand across her eyes and lifted her chin. "I never realized that he . . ."

"Come, we'll not waste words on him. We've more important matters to discuss." He flushed. "That old harridan knows your people, then?"

"Yes."

"And she'll not refrain from spreading tales, I fancy."

Kitty stiffened. She had not thought of the full range of ways in which Mrs. Heath would employ her vicious tongue. The old woman had always disliked and resented Adeline Maynard—Kitty remembered her recent criticism of her mother's remarriage. She would be only too happy to share this gossip with her friends. The tale of Kitty's supposed fall from virtue would be bruited throughout the district—even farther, for she had friends in many southern communities. Kitty blanched. She would be truly disgraced.

"I see by your expression that I am right. Of course

I am right; she will talk." As Kitty nodded, he continued: "And none will give you the benefit of the doubt. None will believe you innocent." He sighed. "My poor girl, it is all my fault. I was sadly foxed last night. I—"

"Please," she interrupted. "I have no blame for you. You were kindness itself and you saved me from those soldiers, whether anyone believes it or not. Furthermore, if I'd not shed so many foolish tears, you'd not felt it incumbent upon yourself to give me comfort and we . . . we'd not been together in the night." She felt her cheeks grow hot.

"My dear," he said gently. "No matter what the circumstances, the evil's done for you, at least. You would be pilloried were you to return, and for naught." He paused, frowning. Then, hesitantly, he continued: "Our countries are at war. The cause, however, is political and does not concern either one of us. Do you agree?"

"Oh, yes," she said, "I—I cannot think on you as—the enemy."

A slight smile twitched the corners of his mouth and was gone. "Nor I you. Yet through my actions, I have brought disgrace upon you, and that is wrong. You are a brave young woman. You deserve respect—you are entitled to it. It is in my power to see that you receive it. I think that you must forget the differences of our nations and . . . accept my name."

"Your name?"

" 'Tis all I can do by way of reparation. I cannot say I love you, but I do like you. And I . . . think we might deal well together, you and I."

She regarded him in amazement. "You . . . you are not *offering* for me!" she exclaimed.

"I am," he said firmly. " 'Tis obvious that you are gently bred. I could not leave you to face the storms that old witch will raise."

"I could go home," she said, knowing she could not go home—not ever again.

"I think we have agreed that it would be most difficult for you to return home with those two near you. Your father's dead, I think?"

"Yes."

"Your mother?"

"She's wed again." She could not restrain a shudder.

His arm tightened. "Ah, that's the way of it. A stepfather?"

She nodded. "We are not . . . friendly."

"I know how that can be." His mouth was suddenly grim. "I had a stepmother and bought colors to escape her. You may not do the same, poor girl, but will you share my colors? The life I offer you will not be easy, though I have heard it will not be a long war. Still, war is war and in casting your lot with mine, you'll need to leave your country. You must note that I do not say you must doff your allegiance, but this grows complicated. My dear, I beg that you will marry me."

She was silent, thinking of Robert—no, not of Robert; he did not loom as large in her thoughts as her stepfather and his brother. She looked at the man beside her. She liked his face: it was a handsome face and there was strength as well as beauty in it—worth more than either, there was kindness. She did not love him, nor he her, but suddenly a future spent facing those who would look upon her with the contempt shown by Mrs. Heath, or with the knowing smiles she had seen in the eyes of the young corporal, was too much to contemplate. "I . . . I will marry you," she said shyly. "And I do thank you for . . . offering for me."

His look was serious and relieved. "I thank you for accepting me. If you'd not allowed me to atone for my

63

folly of the night, I fear the burden of guilt would have been hard for me to bear."

"But there is no guilt," she could not help asserting.

"Enough," he said. "There might well have been. I cannot deny that once I'd taken you in my arms, I could not bring myself to let you go. I needed the comfort that you brought me—I wanted you near me, and indeed I was tempted to . . . possess you. That, I fear, is the truth, my dear."

She dropped her eyes. "It was a strange, terrible night: the flames, the winds, the smoke . . ."

"Terrible," he agreed. "Do you know—" he paused and looked at her with a rueful little smile—"I've not your name."

"It's Katherine Maynard, but I am really known as Kitty; at least I prefer it so."

"Of course. Kitty suits you."

She looked up at him. "And besides the Major and the Quentin, you are . . . ?"

"Gareth and several more besides—but Gareth's how I am called."

"Gareth Quentin," she repeated. "But what a lovely name!"

"I am pleased that you will bear it, too."

"Oh." She blinked back tears. "I . . . I shall try to be a good wife to you." It seemed to her that he tensed and, for a moment, she had the feeling that in some way he had withdrawn from her. Then, smiling, he rose and held out his hands to her. "Come, we'll need to make arrangements. I imagine the Admiral will wed us!"

Four

Wrapped in a cloak grown shabby through constant wear and a woolen gown that the dashing Miss Kitty Maynard of The Oaks would have scorned to present to her abigail, Kitty Quentin came reluctantly forth from the tiny cabin she and her husband occupied upon the brig *Ajax,* bound for the port of Dublin, and stood at the half-open door. She called back to Mrs. Briggs, the wife of the first mate, "Please watch him carefully and if he wakes and wonders where I am, tell him I shall be back momentarily."

"Now don't you fret, love." Mrs. Briggs, fair, plump and good-natured, her face weathered from many voyages, regarded Kitty fondly. " 'Tain't right for you to be cooped up so long in the cabin. It's fresh air you need, else you'll be took sick too. I'll ease his mind, poor dear."

Kitty gave her a brief smile. "Tell him I'll be back in an instant."

"Longer'n that," the woman insisted. "It's a fair shame you got so much on your shoulders, an' you but a slip of a girl. I could wish that Briggs wasn't bound in the opposite direction, for I'd like us to see you 'ome."

"You're very kind, but I shall manage. And sure you and your husband are not ashore long enough to spend your time caring for us. You've already been so helpful; I don't know what we should have done without you."

"Tush." The woman flushed red. " 'Tweren't noth-in'. Now go along with you. There's a strong breeze an' it looks like we might 'ave a bit o' weather afore long."

As she hurried along the narrow companionway, Kitty found the ship beginning to heave under her feet. Fortunately, after a month and a half at sea, she could keep her balance. In a few moments she was on deck. Moving to the side of the vessel, she clutched the wet ropes and stared into the darkness. Late that afternoon, the lookout had cried, "Land ho," but at present she could see only the waters, dark under a sickle moon and a sky with stars that were being rapidly obscured by masses of wind-driven clouds. She suspected that there might be more than a "bit o' weather," possibly a storm; and, the air being chill, there could even be snow.

Mrs. Briggs had expected it long before now and had described a voyage she had made the previous year, when icicles had hung from the rigging and glittered in the masts. " 'Twere a rare, pretty sight," she had said. It was one that Kitty was heartily glad they had been spared; it would have impeded their progress and it was imperative that Gareth be home as soon as possible.

Tightening her hold on the ropes, Kitty braced herself against the rolling motion of the ship. The wind was growing stronger and the waves were rising. She swal-

lowed nervously, but there was no ridding herself of the
constriction in her throat. She had no trouble guessing its
origin. She was frightened. It was, however, a different
fear from that which had possessed her when they had
brought Gareth back from the battlefield, his arm hanging
limp at his side and the surgeon talking gravely about
amputation. Fortunately, there had been no need for that,
but the healing process would be long and the General
had decreed that he must be sent back to England. They
would be going to Ramsdale, Quentin's home in a part of
the country known as Dorset.

Ramsdale in Dorset. In the last month, it had
seemed as remote and unreal as a mountain on the moon.
Now . . . The constriction in her throat seemed to increase
as, superimposed upon the darkness ahead, she envisioned the outlines of a Norman castle—or rather the
moat, now filled in, the walls and the keep, all that
remained of the original building. In the years following
its construction, it had undergone many changes.

"You will find Gothic, Tudor, Jacobean and even a
dash of Queen Anne in its storied halls," Gareth had
laughed. "And before my stepmother died, I understand
from my sister that she had a ruined temple constructed
in the gardens."

Kitty had heard about the estate in the hours preced-
ing their wedding when, shy and trembling, a condition
she had never experienced until then, she had accompanied him aboard H.M.S. *Iphegenia,* one of the British
flotilla anchored in Chesapeake Bay, he having obtained
permission from a surprised and disapproving commander
to bring her with him.

By a great stroke of luck, they had left Washington
an hour ahead of a devastating hurricane which, in the
two hours of its duration, had leveled numerous houses
and scattered the invading British army. Impossible to

know the fate of Robert and his mother, who might have been buried in the ruins of their house. She wrenched her thoughts away from the pair of them. To think of Robert was to wonder why she had ever imagined herself in love with him. The characteristics he had displayed upon that terrible morning must have been inherent in his nature—indeed, looking back on their childhood, she could remember instances when he had not been as brave as she had expected him to be. That time, for instance, when he was sure there had been Indians lurking in the woods. He had spurred and kicked his horse until it had reared and tossed him from its back. A frightened Kitty, seeing him pale and unconscious, had forgotten all about the reasons for his accident.

"Some day the scales will fall away from your eyes . . ."—who had told her that? Yes, Rayburn Abbott. She recalled her indignation at the aspersions he had cast on Robert. She was still indignant but for a different reason —*he* had seen through Robert and she had not. Of course she had been younger then. She felt as though, in the last five months, she had aged as many years.

It had been a very difficult time for her, being an American aboard an enemy ship, particularly *Iphegenia*, where she had been with people who were sure they knew the reasons behind Major Quentin's hasty marriage. That had not been the worst of it. The British had suffered appalling losses, including that of General Ross, the man who had directed the burning of Washington.

According to Gareth, Ross, setting out to capture the key city of Maryland, had said, "I will eat supper in Baltimore or in Hell."

Bullets from the muskets of three young American militiamen, positioned in a tree over Ross's cavalcade, had prevented the General from enjoying that meal—at least in Baltimore. His death had saddened and confused his men. His troops had retreated from Baltimore after failing to destroy Fort McHenry with their fiery rockets. The British had subsequently engaged in a series of skirmishes along the shores of Chesapeake Bay which had left their ranks even more depleted. That, together with the unrelenting summer heat, the mosquitoes, the fever and the dysentery, had rendered the survivors miserable and resentful. Their collective rancor had been visited upon Kitty; it was almost as though in her small person, she embodied all America. Since she could not help secretly rejoicing over her country's triumphs in the face of so well-disciplined an army, she was uncomfortably aware that their bitterness was not without foundation. Furthermore, though he had never said as much, she had feared that Gareth, despite his unfailing courtesy and kindness, also resented her—but for a different reason.

In telling her of Ramsdale, of his late stepmother, and his younger sister Serena, he had hesitatingly explained that he held the title of Viscount. Even more hesitatingly he had mentioned that he had been betrothed to a young woman with the odd name of Dillian Vennor. The daughter of an old, distinguished but impoverished family, her dwindling estate had adjoined that of Ramsdale.

Kitty had not failed to note the similarity to her own situation with Robert. But there had been one difference: Dillian Vennor's parents had provided a haven for two very lonely children. Gareth's mother had died soon after the birth of Serena. The little girl had been but one and her brother five when Lord Ramsdale, their father, had remarried. The new Lady Ramsdale, a spoiled beauty, had cared to live only in their London house, where she might reign as a brilliant Whig hostess. Her stepchildren remained in the country. Bereft of both parents —for, at the behest of his wife, Lord Ramsdale became immersed in politics—the two of them were remanded to the indifferent care of a series of governesses, tutors and nurses. Their only experience of family life was with the Vennor children, John, David and Dillian. They had become very close and eventually the Ramsdale children spent more time at the Vennor estate than at home, particularly after the birth of Lionel, Gareth's half-brother.

Kitty frowned as she recalled Gareth's diffident description of Lady Ramsdale's concentrated efforts to discredit him in the eyes of his father. Since the man was deeply in love with his beautiful wife, she had had little difficulty in persuading him of Gareth's deficiencies. Possessed of a kindness that had kept him from enjoying hunting or, when he was in London, cockfighting and bearbaiting, he had been considered effeminate by his father. His love of books and study had been derided. It had been partially to prove himself a man that Gareth had become a lieutenant in the Horse Guards. He had been in Spain when he had heard of Lionel's death: the boy had succumbed to a chill caught while salmon fishing in Scotland. It had been the first in a series of deaths. His father had been killed in a coaching accident, and shortly after Gareth had left for America, his stepmother had died of a female complaint.

In describing these happenings, Gareth had smiled ruefully. "My sister and I, you see, live charmed lives, and you will be spared the hostility of a mother-in-law, more attractive than Mrs. Heath but much like her as far as temperament goes. I think you will like my little sister—not so little now, for she is out of the schoolroom and spends a great deal of her time in London, where she is determined to make a great splash!"

Kitty swallowed again but the lump in her throat would not go away. It was pleasant to think that few obstacles awaited her in England but the one remaining was, by far, the most intimidating. That, of course, was the Honorable Dillian Vennor. She recoiled from contemplating the girl's despair on reading the letter Gareth had despatched, informing her of his marriage to an American. She imagined that her unhappiness must increase tenfold when he brought his alien, enemy bride back to Ramsdale. That, however, was only part of her fear—the other part concerned Gareth's own reactions.

A vivid image of the early days of their marriage came back to her: she would as lief dismiss it, but she could not. At that period, Gareth had withdrawn from her and she from him. Once they had been joined in holy wedlock, it had been as if—honor being satisfied, his main duty toward her was discharged. On their first evening together, he had said hesitantly, "My dear, it were best, I believe, if . . . if we came to know each other better ere assuming the . . . obligations attendant upon marriage."

She, who had been intimidated by the thought of those same obligations, had readily and thankfully agreed. It had not been a happy period. Gareth had been polite but distant and, she was sure, very unhappy. For her part, there had been the memory of Robert.

Oddly enough, despite her contempt for his cowardly actions, despite her prompt disavowal of any lingering affection for him, she had thought about him far more often than she had expected to. Mainly, she had dwelt upon the times when they were little. They had enjoyed a warm friendship in those days, and though its memory had been tarnished by his recent conduct, it had been very difficult to forget him. Lying on a narrow cot in the minute cabin she shared with Gareth, she had often dreamed of Robert. She was sure that her husband, tossing restlessly on a similar cot, had been devoting most

71

of his thoughts to the Honorable Dillian and no doubt bemoaning the fact that he had, in a sense, betrayed her. Given his strong sense of honor, that belief must have increased his misery. On those nights, regret had followed regret. If she had not come to Washington to seek out Robert—if she had not gone up on the roof—if she had not tried to get the attention of the soldiers—if Gareth had not been foxed, then . . . But it had been of no use to dwell on the past. All that counted was her present situation—legally tied to a man she did not love.

The *débacle* at Fort McHenry had altered that situation. Gareth, returning to the warship, miserable over the loss of so many troops, so many comrades, had looked at her in despair. Impossible not to comfort him, then. Impossible not to put her arms around him and hold him close, though feeling all the while that she was naught but a surrogate for the Honorable Dillian, while he—was he Robert? She had not been sure . . . and then all her thoughts had been suspended as he had become, in fact as well as name, her husband. She had been confused and frightened at first, but soon she had responded to his needs and much to her surprise, she had discovered that their physical communion had helped to alleviate her own woes. It had seemed to have a similar effect upon him. They had fallen asleep in each other's arms, awakening in the night to love again, clinging to each other with a desperation that had in it, as much anguish as passion.

In the morning their old constraints had vanished— though not altogether. She had found herself in love with him, only to see him withdraw again. Another frustrating week had passed, a week in which she had joined the other women aboard the ship in helping the overburdened doctors care for the wounded.

Gareth had not wanted her to mix with those women, many of whom were whores from the docks, cohabiting with crew members. However, the once independent and still headstrong Miss Maynard of The Oaks had insisted. Kitty had wanted to feel useful, and it had also served to ease her awkward position, particularly since she had proved an efficient and, to her own surprise, detached nurse. She had been able to minister sympathetically but not hysterically to men who endured agonies even worse than those they had sustained on the battlefield as surgeons hacked off limbs and cauterized wounds with naught but draft of spirits to dull the pain.

The work had taken its toll at night, when her dreams had been haunted by the horrors that had filled her days. At such moments, she had sobbed into her pillow and longed to feel her husband's arms around her, but Gareth, sleeping alone on his cot, had barely a look for her until the day Captain Richard Powis, his best friend, had been blown to pieces less than three feet away from him.

He had come shuddering back to the ship and again there had been that desperate, wordless, reaching out. After that, all constraints had dropped: each time he had been able to rejoin her, there had been a passionate reunion. It had no longer seemed merely a question of expediency for one night; holding her close against him, he had murmured, "My dearest, dearest Kitty, I do thank God for you. You've been my salvation and are my true, my only love."

Luxuriating in his embrace, she had replied, "And you, my own, are mine . . . forsaking all others."

"Forsaking all others," he had murmured solemnly, "until death do us part." In those moments, the wedding ceremony which had once held so little meaning for them, had become the binding tie it had been meant to be.

Three days after this revelation, he had been brought back to the *Iphegenia*—on a plank.

Sobs shook Kitty. It had been an agony she would never forget, seeing him so pale, so blood-stained. It had been a worse misery to witness his pain and his eventual fever. Loving him as much as she did, she would have given her heart to have changed places with him. The fever had eventually yielded to her careful nursing and spent itself, but he had been weak and listless. He was still weak, though his arm was mending and the sabre cut on the side of his hip nearly healed. Indeed, she was sure that once he was home, his health must improve rapidly. She was anxious that he get there, but would the Honorable Dillian come to see him—Dillian, upon whom he, in the depths of his delirium, had called incessantly. He had babbled of fields in spring, of billowing rain clouds as they rode together on the downs, of gathering black currants in the hedgerows, of plighting their troth in the moonlight.

It was true that once he had regained his senses, he had been very loving, very tender, very grateful—so loving that she could almost believe Dillian had not existed, but she had, she did, lurking at the back of his mind, and possibly awaiting him in Dorset. What would his feelings be when he saw her again? Would he resent his wife? Would he grow indifferent to her once more?

As these fears crossed her mind, she chided herself. With his highly-developed sense of honor and duty, he could never be totally indifferent. He would be good to her; yet, all the time, she would know that he was yearning for Dillian Vennor while she, Kitty Quentin, loved him with a passion she had never imagined she would experience.

"It's time and past that you became a young lady, Kitty Maynard."

That had been the observation of Wellington Abbott

on the day he had met her riding across the fields, astride and bareback. An image of herself, as she had been then, leaped into her mind. She had been wearing breeches, borrowed from a cousin staying at The Oaks. Her red curls had been wild about her perspiring face. She had glared at him furiously, defiantly, longing to slash his face with her riding crop. She had been, she realized regretfully, the very picture of mutinous, undisciplined childhood. Much as she hated to admit it, he had been right to scold her. She had certainly not thought so at the time and she had been most put out with her mother for agreeing with him. She had accused Adeline of not loving her any more.

Kitty shook her head wonderingly. That episode had taken place shortly before she had run away. In less than five months, she had become a totally different person. However, she had not been changed into a "young lady." Though her nineteenth birthday was nearly a half a year away, she had already matured into a woman, one who could be heartily glad that Gareth Quentin had never made the acquaintance of the spoiled, foolish girl she had been. He would not have admired tempestuous, impulsive Kitty Maynard. He wanted a womanly woman. He wanted the Honorable Dillian Vennor. She grimaced. She must expel this fear, or at least place it in the proper perspective. Gareth had been wed a little over four months; he had been betrothed to Dillian Vennor for two years and had known her all his life. His desertion of her must have preyed on his mind—yes, even after he had become reconciled to his bride. Naturally, when stricken with fever, his old guilts had reasserted themselves. It was wrong, Kitty told herself, to resent poor Dillian Vennor, to wish that she had never existed, to pray that she had found consolation quickly, to hope that she had moved far, far away from Ramsdale. Kitty expelled a quavering sigh, and then her worries were abruptly dispersed by a heave of the vessel and an onrush of water that drenched her from head to foot, while above her, the sky seemed almost to have been cleft in twain by a searing blue white bolt of lightning, followed immediately by thunder so loud that she was momentarily deafened. Rain, sheets of it, began to fall, while Kitty, terrified, clung to the ropes, wincing as their rough hairy surfaces scraped against her palms.

The vessel heaved again, gained the top of a veritable mountain of a wave and dropped down into a dark valley of choppy waters. Around her, various objects rattled, slithered across the deck while the air was filled with the roar of the elements and the yelling of the crew. A tall figure in a dripping slicker loomed up beside her. " 'Ere," he shouted, "wot ye be doin' out 'ere?" Before she could scream a reply, he had slipped and fallen. To her horror, he was borne toward the side of the ship which, at that moment, listed so that he was thrown overboard into the roiling waters, his cry lost amidst the shrieking winds.

Trembling and in tears, she cast a look in the direction of the companionway and longed to rush back to Gareth's side; but she dared not make the attempt lest she follow the hapless seaman to share his doom. She clung even more tightly to the ropes, vaguely aware of shouted orders concerning the securing of the sails. Shapes, rain-blurred, ran up and down the deck. An accident, similar to that which she had witnessed, must have taken place on the quarter-deck, for she heard another agonized scream issuing from that direction, but she hardly attended it—she was thinking only of Gareth and actively resenting Mrs. Briggs for having persuaded her to leave his side. She had not needed the air. She was used to foul odors and close quarters. He must have awakened by now, and no doubt he was frantic with worry. He had grown very dependent upon her. She cast another frenzied look at the companionway, her apprehension increasing. How long would the storm continue? There had to be an end to it. It had come up so quickly; it must dissipate as quickly, please God!

It did blow itself out in short order, as all squalls must, and despite the continued pitching and tossing of the craft, Kitty was able to reach the companionway. As she went down the steps, she found herself increasingly frightened. It had been a fearful tempest; one of the masts had cracked. Water had seeped into the bowels of the ship, and stepping into the corridor, she found it above her ankles. She was afraid to contemplate what might have taken place in their cabin. Had Mrs. Briggs remained with him, or had she hastened back to her own husband? No, the first mate would have been on deck and she would not have left Gareth alone. She was a responsible person and . . . Kitty's fear's intensified as she saw a door swinging open in front of her. She did not want it to be the door to their cabin—but it was!

"Mrs. Briggs!" she cried, as she hurried ahead.

There was no answer. Reaching the cabin, she bit back a scream. Mrs. Briggs lay unconscious just inside the door, and near her, fallen from his bunk was Gareth. With a sob, Kitty edged carefully around the mate's wife and knelt beside him. She felt his wrist. To her relief, she found the pulse still beating strongly, but he, too, was unconscious, a thin stream of blood streaked his forehead. She could guess the agony that must result from such a fall, and was almost glad that he had had some surcease from his suffering.

Toward noon of the next day, under a sky so dark and murky that it seemed as if the sun had already set, the *Ajax* limped into port at Dublin Bay, and Kitty, sitting beside Gareth's bunk, whispered into his unheeding ear, "We're in Ireland, my own darling, and in a matter of a few days only you will be back at Ramsdale."

Gently, she pushed the dark hair back from his pale forehead, trying to quell her panic. He had received a sharp blow on the head and the ship's doctor had diagnosed a concussion resulting in coma. He had not been able to tell her when Gareth might awaken.

Tears filled her eyes and she blinked them back. It was no use weeping. All the tears in the world would not atone for the fact, that against her better judgment, she had left his side. If she had not gone, she might have been able to push him back in his bunk and he would not have sustained this new hurt.

"Oh, Gareth," she whispered brokenly, "will you ever forgive me?"

But of course, she told herself, he would forgive her and assure her that it was not her fault—which, in a sense, it was not, for she had not left him alone and certainly she could not have guessed that Mrs. Briggs would be hit by a falling life-preserver and knocked unconscious though not, thank God, badly hurt. If Kitty had been with him, it was possible that she might have suffered a similar injury—no, she did not believe that. She was smaller and more agile . . . He groaned. She tensed as she bent over him. His eyes were open!

"Gareth," she cried. "Oh, thank God, you are awake. Oh, my dearest, I . . ."

"W-where am I?" His query cut across her protestations. His eyes were wide and staring, yet he did not seem to see her.

He was confused, she decided. "You fell from your bunk last night during that dreadful storm and—"

"Storm . . . bunk . . . I . . . I am on a ship," he said falteringly.

"Yes." His question disturbed her. Had he suffered a recurrence of his fever? She put her hand on his forehead and found it cool. Striving to keep her voice steady, she added, "You are aboard the *Ajax* but we've just reached Dublin. You will soon be home."

"R-Ramsdale," he murmured.

"Yes," she said, breathing a sigh of relief. "We are finally back in your country—or very near it."

He stared at her. "I feel very weak. Have I been ill?"

Her trepidation returned. "Yes, my dear, you were wounded."

He frowned. "Odd—I do not remember that. I expect it was at Burgos?"

"Burgos!" she repeated blankly.

He did not appear to have heard her. His eyes had strayed from her face. "Are we far from Ramsdale?"

"I . . . I understand it's not more than a few days' journey."

"Good. My fiancée must be worrying, but thank God, I'll be able to see her soon. I've been wounded badly?" His tone was anxious. "Are . . . are my limbs intact?"

She nodded. She could not speak. She was beginning to understand what had happened to him.

"Ah," he sighed. "That is well. I'd come back to my Dillian a whole man. And you . . ." He regarded her questioningly, "who are you, my child?"

"Kitty," she managed to whisper.

"Ah, one of the sailors' women set to nurse me, no

79

doubt? I hope you've not been much burdened with me, my girl. But never fear. I'll see you well rewarded for your pains."

Because it might be dangerous to disillusion him, dangerous to let him know the truth at this moment, she said merely, "I thank you, sir."

Five

Dorset in early January. It seemed to Kitty, bracing herself against the motion of the coach bearing herself and Gareth over the muddy, crooked road that would ultimately bring them to Ramsdale, that she had heard her father describe this month as being particularly bleak in the British Isles. A week of seeing vast, snow-covered fields, groves of bare, twisted trees and ice-sheathed lakes, the whole under a sullen gray sky, had led her to agree with him.

She looked out the window to where a flock of sheep was wending their way slowly through the snow. She shivered, and wondered why they did not freeze. Despite the fact that she was wrapped in a warm lap-robe, a deep cold such as she had never experienced penetrated the crevices of the vehicle to chill her. Yet, it seemed less frigid than the cold that entered her heart each time she glanced at the profile of the man sitting beside her. His eyes were shut and he huddled in his corner; he was seemingly asleep, but she, who knew so much about him, knew he was not sleeping.

Judging from the puzzled frown that came and went on his brow, she supposed that he was still trying to recollect those events that had culminated in this journey back to his estate with a stranger whom he must needs call wife. Though no complaint had passed his lips, she feared he must be in pain. The fall that had caused his loss of memory had shaken him badly and for the first three days on the road he had been lying on a litter propped between the two seats of the carriage. On the fourth day, he had insisted that he was well enough to sit up, and so he had remained: either silently staring out of the window, sleeping, or feigning sleep. He had spoken to her as little as possible and she was sure that his every thought was centered on the Honorable Dillian Vennor.

Unwillingly, Kitty recalled his horror and what had seemed almost a physical agony when, with the help of Mrs. Briggs and the ship's doctor, she had managed to convince him that, rather than being invalided home from Burgos in Northern Spain in 1812, it was 1815 and he on his way back from America with his wife!

At first he had feared that Dillian was dead. Assured that she was not, he had looked blankly at Kitty, asking her if his fiancée had wed another? To her negative answer, his puzzled look, his agonized queries had engendered an answering agony in her own heart, and at the same time, an amazement that, feeling as he had about the Honorable Dillian Vennor, he had offered for her. She also feared that despite all he had told her concerning his growing affection and eventual love for herself, he might have been lying both to her and himself—trying, indeed, to make the best of a bad situation. And, she mused, he had succeeded—at least as far as she was concerned. He was all she wanted and, she thought with a throb of terror, he was all she had!

If Mrs. Heath had survived the hurricane—and somehow she had the feeling that it would take more than a mere windstorm to topple that lady—she would have apprised her family of Kitty's misadventure with a British soldier. She would tell the story in such a way as would make it seem entirely Kitty's fault. Her stepfather would not hesitate to turn the tale to his own advantage and might even succeed in alienating her mother's love.

She had written to her mother explaining what had happened, but was not sure the letter had reached her. She had also sent her another letter from Dublin, giving her her direction in Dorset; there might be mail awaiting her at Ramsdale, but she feared that this was a vain hope. Under the circumstances, she, a wealthy heiress, whose father's will had provided her with monies apart from her dowry, was totally dependent upon this stranger.

If only his memory would return! The doctor's words came back to her.

"There's no telling when he'll recover from this affliction, Lady Quentin. It might be a day, it might be weeks or even years."

"Or . . . never?" she had asked.

"I do not believe that could happen, but the condition varies from person to person." He had spoken coldly, disinterestedly. He did not like her. She was an American, he seemed to be thinking, and should have remained in her own country.

She had encountered that attitude at inns all along the roads. Her accent had aroused frowns and glares. She could not blame them. Despite the treaty signed at Ghent the day before Christmas, the English were looking back on two years of fighting that had left their ranks far more depleted than those of her people. It was only at the Royal Crown, the hostelry in which they had spent the previous night that the name "Quentin of Ramsdale" had bathed her in a magical glow.

Hostile stares had been supplanted by twinkles, dour faces had broken into broad grins, maids were sent scurrying off to prepare their chamber, hot possets had been offered and the landlord bent double, bowing. His lady had given them the very best room, and at Kitty's request, put in a cot for her, since by the nature of his wounds, her husband must sleep alone.

In lieu of a valet, Gareth was dependent upon her, his left arm still in a sling. However, he had not suffered her presence in his chamber gladly nor welcomed the intimate services she needed to perform for him.

A bitter smile played about her mouth as she recalled her forlorn hope that his first night ashore might bring a lifting of the dark cloud that had fallen over his memory. It had been obviated when the first rays of feeble winter sunshine had revealed to a wakeful Kitty, his unhappy face and his accusing stare.

Though she had explained the circumstances attendant upon their marriage, she feared he might not believe her. He might even believe she had trapped him into this marriage. He would certainly never credit the one fact she had withheld from him, that he had learned to love her. She could not blame him. The long voyage, coupled with her constant attendance upon him, had taken its toll of her appearance. Her mirror showed her that she was too thin and too pale. Her hair had lost its bright lustre and in want of Becky Lou's ministrations, she wore it gathered into a simple but often untidy knot at the back of her neck. Grief had dulled her eyes, etched dark circles under them. Furthermore, her clothes were shabby;

she had only two woollen gowns and a cloak, all hastily purchased at a shop where ready-made garments could be found. All in all, she thought drearily, she looked twice her age and if anyone from home had seen her, they would never have guessed that this drab little woman had once been pretty Kitty Maynard, the belle of Fairfax County.

Tears threatened, but enough of her old spirit remained for her to blink them back ruthlessly. He must not see her weeping! It would only depress him. Yet it was very hard to be stoical in view of the situation. It could have been such a happy homecoming for them both . . . .

Kitty pressed her face against the window, then stiffened. They had turned off the highway and were in a heavily wooded region where on either side of them rose tall, winter-stripped beech trees. She remembered that Gareth had mentioned an avenue of beeches lining the road that ran through the park adjoining Ramsdale. Were they nearing his home? She had no notion of the time. Mrs. Greaves, the landlady at the Royal Crown, had promised to send a messenger to alert the occupants of the estate to their impending arrival.

"You'll be there in less than four hours, Milady," she had said.

Four hours? Had they been traveling that long? Her heart began to pound. In addition to her other worries, she was about to enter her husband's home—and who would be there to receive her? His sister? The Honorable Dillian Vennor, as well? No, she could not bear to imagine that! She shrank into her corner, wishing she dared to instruct the coachman to turn back and drive . . . where? Nowhere! Her fright was rendering her selfish. Gareth's welfare must come first with her. She was sure that some of his depression would lift once he had returned to his estate. But she could not think of the future, not yet.

They had passed a small, gray house—a gatehouse. As the coachman reined in the horses, she placed a steadying hand on Gareth's arm and inwardly quailed as she felt him wince at her unwelcome touch.

There was a tap at the window. Glancing to the side, she met the inquiring stare of a tall, elderly man in plum-colored livery. His eyes slipped past her and brightened; with a broad smile and a touch of his forelock, he waved them onward.

She had a brief glimpse of a broad, snowy expanse dotted by pines and skeletal trees for which she had no name; seconds later, they passed into a huge courtyard and halted once more. The door beside her was opened by a footman in the same livery as that worn by the gatekeeper. Stepping carefully down the steps he had provided for her, Kitty had a vague impression of a jumble of tall, gray stone buildings with snowy roofs. Fortunately, the snow in the courtyard had been shoveled to one side and she could easily make her way to the other side of the coach where two footmen were assisting Gareth to descend. As he stood, looking about him, a girl dashed toward him crying joyfully and at the same time tearfully, "Gareth, Gareth, Gareth!"

For the first time since they had left the ship, he smiled. "Serena!" He reached out his good arm and like a homing bird she flew into it, but Kitty was quick to see that it was a very careful flight and that it ended with her sustaining arm around his waist.

Their reunion, though joyful, seemed tinged with an unspoken regret as sister stared into brother's eyes. Watching them, Kitty felt cold—colder than the day, which was chill enough, and colder than the stone beneath her feet, frigid from the snow which must have lain upon it until recently cleared away. There should have been another come to greet him and her absence seemed to make her presence more defined. Kitty wondered if Dillian Vennor had been notified of Gareth's return.

Serena moved away from her brother and looked at Kitty, who returned her gaze with interest. Viewed fully for the first time, the Honorable Serena Quentin's resemblance to her brother lay mainly in her dark hair and deep blue eyes. Her features were less classic—her mouth was too wide, her nose slightly *retroussé*—but, if she were pretty rather than beautiful, her attraction lay in a liveliness of expression which, though muted now, was not entirely in abeyance. Kitty remembered Gareth telling her that Serena could be, on occasion, very mischievous. Lovingly, he had recounted some of her scrapes, and, seeing her, Kitty had no trouble believing him. For the rest, she was tall and the dark cloak she clutched about her caused her to appear very slender. She said, "You must be my brother's wife."

Had her tone been vaguely hostile? Kitty was not sure, for, coinciding with his sister's question, was his low-voiced introduction. "My dear, this is Serena . . . Serena, my love, this is Katherine."

Kitty grew even colder. He had taken to calling her "Katherine" as if he felt "Kitty" too intimate a form of address for him to employ when addressing a woman who was, to all intents and purposes, a stranger. In view of this attitude, she was glad she had had the foresight to beg Mrs. Greaves to include a description of Gareth's condition in the message she had sent to the castle. Her face felt frozen, but she managed a smile. "I am happy to meet you. I have heard so much about you." Oddly, she almost felt as if she were lying and feared he must believe that in fact she was for all that he had told her about his bright, gay, charming young sister, for whom he cherished so deep an affection, had been divulged while they were yet in America.

"I know you will love her as I do," he had said. "And I know she'll adore you, once she gets to know you." He had ended that prophecy with a kiss. Kitty, confronted with this memory, envied that other self, that girl who had been so very happy in her new-found love, so unconscious of the chasm which would open before her.

Serena, meanwhile, was saying, "I've waited long to meet you—certainly you have figured largely in Gareth's letters. But—" she looked anxiously at her brother—"It's chilly out here—do let us go indoors."

"Yes," Kitty said hastily, glad that the subject had been turned from letters he would not remember having written. "Gareth is still not himself. He should go to bed at once."

"I think," he said, "that it is up to me to determine that, my dear." His eyes, cold as they had rested on her, warmed when they fell on his sister's face. "I must make acquaintance with Ramsdale again. I pray there have not been as many changes as you mentioned when last you wrote."

Serena regarded him in surprise and bit her lip as his condition was fully revealed to her. However, with an admirable casualness, she replied, "No, and those our late stepmother made, I have rectified in part, though of course I could do nothing about the Folly in the garden."

For the first time, his laughter rang out. "Folly upon folly, but you've made me easier in my mind. I should have had more confidence in your making things right and tight again."

"Yes, you should," she returned, "for this I will always do as far as I am able."

Serena had kept her eyes fixed on her brother, but Kitty, hearing those words felt that they were tinged with a regret which must grow even greater when the girl learned how his heart yet yearned for Dillian Vennor. As his fiancée's good friend, she could have no liking for the woman who had supplanted her. Kitty shivered, saying almost defiantly, "I vow, the cold out here is attacking my very vitals. Please, do let us go inside."

"Of course," Serena said quickly. "Come."

Once Gareth had told Kitty, "I long to show you my home, my dearest and until I can carry you across its threshold as my bride, I'll not think us wholly joined."

As it happened, Kitty walked across that same threshold and the only reminder of that joining took place when the tall, elderly woman, introduced to her as Mrs. Blaney, the housekeeper, said, "I bid you welcome, Lady Quentin."

"Does Milady wish anything more?"

"No thank you, Mary, that will be all." Kitty forced a smile as she dismissed the abigail sent to her chamber to oversee preparations for the bath she had requested.

"Yes, Milady." Mary, a thin, pale girl of perhaps eighteen, clad in a print dress and a mob cap, curtseyed and hurried from the room but not before Kitty had glimpsed a look of amusement in her narrow, lashless blue eyes.

Kitty's hand clenched into a fist; she had a strong desire to hit the girl which, of course, was wholly reprehensible. She had never hurt a servant and never would. However, Mary had annoyed her from the moment she had stepped into the room with her armful of towels. Her whole attitude had been one of exaggerated humility and it had not been difficult for Kitty to guess that she, secure in her belief that this shabby young woman from what she must yet consider "the colonies," was unused to dealing with servants. It was a belief which must have been strengthened when Kitty had dismissed her without availing herself of her aid in undressing or in the bath. Her reasons for this lay in the fact that her undergarments were as shabby as her gowns. The strong lye soaps which were all she had been able to obtain on shipboard had played havoc with the thin silks and delicate laces. If Mary had seen them, she would have had even more to confide to her fellow servants. Kitty sighed. Seen through the critical eyes of Serena and the staff, she must appear very much out of place in these luxurious surroundings, and Gareth's attitude could only add more fuel to their burning conjectures.

She glanced at a portrait that hung on the far wall. It depicted a most beautiful lady, her hair powdered and piled high in the style of some fifty years ago. Since her eyes were dark blue and of much the same shape as Gareth's, she was probably his grandmother. Kitty could imagine her in this spacious chamber with its molded ceilings, its walls hung with a blue and silver striped paper, its Louis XV furnishings, its thick Aubusson carpet and silken draperies. She could also imagine her looking down her aristocratic nose at this small, shabby interloper, who would sit on her brocaded chairs and sleep in her huge, canopied bed.

Kitty stared defiantly back at the lady. Her own chamber at home was almost as large and if its furnishings were Chippendale rather than French, they were equally fine, while the garments in her armoire were either copied from the latest fashions or imported from France. If only . . . No, she would not indulge in any more vain regrets! Turning her back on the portrait, she prepared to take her bath.

The tub had been set down near the fireplace. Once

she had stepped into it, her mood improved. The water was just the right temperature. There were lovely scented soaps, a huge sponge and big, thick towels. By the time she had finished her ablutions and dried her hair before the fire, she felt considerably more like herself. The lassitude that had invaded her was gone and she no longer had any need to follow Serena's advice and nap before supper. Instead, she was eager to explore this dwelling, so lovingly described to her by Gareth.

"I long to show you . . ." Kitty shook her head. Gareth would not "long to show her" an abode which he had once hoped to share with his Dillian. However, she would not give in to the pain that could so easily wash over her; that too came under the heading of vain regrets and would wreak havoc with her countenance. Gareth would certainly not appreciate a lugubrious mien this evening; it would make him either guilt-ridden or irritated. Furthermore, she was not willing, for the sake of her own pride, to present him such an image.

She moved to her mirror where she was somewhat reassured by her reflection. Curiosity had always acted as a powerful stimulant upon her spirits—possibly it was that which had brought a sparkle to her eyes. A vigorous brushing had restored some of the lustre to her curls and if she did not look like her old self, at least she was not as depressed and bedraggled as she must have appeared upon arrival.

With a surge of defiance, she whispered, "If Gareth is not content to be my love or my husband, let me be Miss Kitty Maynard once again—and enjoy myself anyway!"

The hall was dark when she emerged. Kitty Maynard would not have cast a wistful glance at the door to Gareth's chamber, which lay just beyond her dressing room—but it was that Kitty who kept her from opening it, just to see if he required anything. He no longer needed such attentions from her, with a large staff of devoted servants to do his bidding.

On the way down the stairs, she noticed a huge window centered by a stained glass design in the form of a heraldic hound surmounted by a shield over which was the motto *Toujours fidèle*.

"Always faithful," she murmured and ruthlessly blinked away a threatening moisture as she mentally added: always faithful to Dillian Vennor. "None of that," she reprimanded herself. She had to remember her new, or rather her old, identity. Tossing her head defiantly, Kitty Maynard ran lightly down the remaining steps, emerging in the hall and pleased to find that it was empty. Gazing about her, she saw three doors, one behind her, one to the right and the other to the left. She smiled. It was an adventure, deciding which door to open first.

Choosing the portal on her left, she opened it and shivered as a rush of cold air enveloped her. She was looking at a huge banqueting hall, dominated by a highly polished table which could easily sit fifty people. On one side of the room was a magnificent sideboard, and on the other, four long windows which probably faced the courtyard, though she could not be sure of that since the draperies were drawn. These were of dark red velvet, heavily fringed with gold. There were paintings on the walls, but in the dimness it was impossible to see them clearly.

The central chamber, also darkened, proved even larger. In the light streaming from a chandelier in the hall, she discovered more paintings hung on damask-covered walls. A ceiling ornamented with intaglios was centered by a fine crystal chandelier and the chairs nearest to the door were covered with tapestry; but again, a prevading chill discouraged her from further exploration.

Bracing herself against another blast of cold air, Kitty tenatively opened the door on the right and was agreeably surprised to feel warmth and hear the crackle of a fire. Candles glowing in sconces and on tables revealed walls lined from floor to ceiling with shelves of books. Coming inside, she looked about her in amazement. Her father had had an extensive library but that which surrounded her was twice as big. The furnishings, however, were similar enough to bring a lump to her throat. In a windowed alcove stood a large, leather-topped desk much like that where her father had worked, and throughout the long room there were deep comfortable chairs and couches. The mantelpiece was of carved marble rather than wood, as at home; a huge canvas hanging over it depicted a family group. Its counterpart at The Oaks had pictured her grandparents and two of their children. Here, two boys, a dog, and a horse were shown. Judging from their garb, the picture had been painted during the reign of Charles I. At the far end of the chamber, a window facing the dimming gardens differed only in size from that at The Oaks.

Kitty's eyes softened. She no longer had the wish to explore further. In this room, she could feel at home. She loved to read and the idea of curling up in one of the big chairs near the fire seemed infinitely beguiling. Moving to the shelves, she scanned the titles, and seeing a volume of Pope, whose verses she had always fancied, had just taken it down when a man's voice said sharply:

"Stay, what are you about?"

Startled, she turned to find a tall, fair-haired young man striding toward her. He coolly appropriated the book, saying, albeit less sharply, "Mrs. Blaney cannot know you are in here . . ." He broke off, staring at her. "I vow, you are a pretty child." He put an arm around her, and pressed a long kiss on her lips.

93

"Oh!" Wrenching herself from his grasp, Kitty slapped him hard across the mouth. "How dare you!" she cried.

His eyes widened. "Why, what have we here? A tigress, I do believe, or perhaps a tiger kitten." Purposefully, he advanced upon her again. "I like a show of spirit, my lass."

She retreated behind a chair. "I think, Sir, you mistake me."

"What's amiss, my good wench, are you of the Methodist persuasion, then? If so, 'tis a sad waste. That lovely mouth was meant for more than hymn-singing."

"I am indeed complimented," Kitty said with exaggerated politeness, "but . . ." She paused as he stepped to her side again. "I pray you will cease these attentions. I do not find them to my liking."

"Hold." He caught her arm. "Who are you?"

"I think that need not concern you, Sir."

Dropping her arm, he flushed. "Good God, you cannot be the new Lady Quentin!"

"I am," she returned coldly.

"Lord in heaven, you are not what I expected," he blurted.

"Evidently." She turned on her heel only to be confronted by him again. "Sir—" she began freezingly.

"Lady Quentin," he interrupted, "this will never do. You must accept my apologies, else Gareth will blow a hole through my head or run a sword into some necessary part of me, and I need hardly tell you that I am mightily opposed to either course of action."

She felt her lips twitch and was annoyed. She should not be smiling at this outrageous young man. She said coldly, "I assure you, Sir, that even were he of such a mind, my husband's hardly in condition to challenge you."

"But—" he assumed a ludicrously mournful expression— "he will improve in health."

Biting back another threatening smile, Kitty said, "Since I do not know your name, I cannot betray you, Sir."

"But you will know it. That is unavoidable. Indeed, if I am to atone for my reprehensible conduct, I think I must present myself. My name's Vennor—David Vennor."

Kitty paled. "You . . . you are related to the Honorable Dillian Vennor?"

"Her brother, but much less honorable. Now, if I were my older brother Daniel, I would be able to give you a different description of myself. I would be noble, upright and a worthy successor to my father—whenever he leaves this world, which I hope will not be for some time—since Daniel is fearfully good and will no doubt read me homilies on my evil ways until I am in my grave."

She had to laugh, but sobered quickly. "Has your sister come with you this day, then?"

"I am glad that you did not ask if my brother had accompanied me. Fortunately, he and my parents are traveling on the continent. Consequently, if my description has made you long to meet him, you are doomed to disappointment—but I think you asked about my sister. No, she is removed to London and is residing, at least for the season, with my elderly and irascible Aunt Hester."

"Oh."

He gave her a searching look. "Now, why should that intelligence occasion such a sigh of relief?"

Kitty flushed. "I assure you . . ." she began and paused as the door to the library was opened wide.

"David," Serena called.

"Good afternoon, my dear," he called back.

"Ah, John said you'd come in here." Serena moving toward them, stopped short. "Katherine!" she exclaimed in surprise. "I felt sure you must be resting."

"I was less weary than I imagined," Kitty explained.

She thought she discerned a slight frown in the girl's eyes but Serena said pleasantly enough, "Have you met or am I to present Mr. Vennor to you?"

"He has already presented himself, my dear, though I thank you for the gesture," David Vennor said with a smile. Moving to Serena's side, he raised her hand to his lips and turned it over, implanting a large smacking kiss upon its palm.

"Oh, I vow!" Blushing, she pulled her hand away and attempted to stare him down, but Kitty noticed that, rather than reproving, her glance was very fond.

He turned back to Kitty. Outrageously, he said, "We've been discussing our favorite scribblers." He shot a glance at the book in his hand. "Among these Lady Quentin numbers Pope. I was telling her that I am an admirer of our mad, bad, and dangerous Lord Byron. And she replied, quite rightly, that our noble Lord owes something of his 'heroic' style to crabbed little Alexander P. These Americans, I find to my surprise, are quite amazingly well-informed, and on all manner of subjects, too." He bowed to Kitty.

This time, Serena achieved a glare. "I pray you, Katherine," she snapped. "Do not listen to him. He is rude, unmannerly, and a seasoned scoundrel!"

"But she already knows that, my unserene Serena and I am in hopes that she will be beneficent and forgive me my sins."

Serena's eyes narrowed. "And what sins might those be?" she demanded suspiciously.

"Of omission not commission, my own."

"Oh, do desist," she said sharply. "I am sure that neither Katherine nor myself is in the mood for your badinage with poor Gareth so ill upstairs."

His smile vanished. "But he is better, is he not? In your message, you gave me to understand that he was improved."

She flushed and looked down at her hands. "Yes, but . . ."

"But?" he prompted.

Watching the play of expressions on Serena's face, Kitty thought she could guess the reasons behind her obvious confusion. They were, she was sure, also the reasons for David Vennor's arrival. Serena must have sent for him, intending to tell him of Gareth's condition. But why such haste? So that he might get word to his sister and summon her home?

Fury thrilled through her. No wonder Serena was disturbed by Kitty's presence in the library. Naturally she did not want to have such a discussion with him now. Yet, even as this suspicion crossed her mind, her common sense arose to refute it. As Gareth had explained, the Vennors were their oldest and closest friends, and judging from Serena's glances, there might even be a deeper understanding between David and herself.

For Kitty's part, she hoped she was mistaken, for, though David Vennor was young, likely not more than twenty-one or two, there were already lines of dissipation traced across his bow; and, judging from her own experience, even maidservants in Serena's own house were fair prey. She flushed, not wanting to think of his kiss—nor did she want to remain where she was not wanted. She said, "No doubt I should have explained at once, Mr. Vennor, my husband has lost his memory—but 'tis a painful subject for me. I—I think Serena'd best give you the particulars of his . . . affliction, if she will. I pray you will excuse me." Without waiting for their response, she hurried from the room.

The tears she had managed to check had started once again, and reaching her chamber, she could not but give way to them. If Dillian was anything like her brother, it was highly probable that she would not hesitate to press her advantage with Gareth. On the other hand, if she had much in common with David, Kitty could not understand how Dillian would warrant such undying devotion. However, it did no good to indulge in fruitless speculation. Only time could provide the answers she required. Kitty heaved a bitter sigh. The time involved could probably be measured in days—those it took for David Vennor's letter to reach London and for Dillian Vennor's coach to bring her back to the estate with lands that adjoined those of Ramsdale.

Six

Maiden Castle. The name suggested a dwelling inhabited by numbers of those distressed damsels King Arthur's questing knights were fond of rescuing. However, as Serena had explained, it was not a real castle but rather an ancient Celtic stronghold, which had fallen to the Romans and had subsequently been occupied by a tribe called the Belgae, of which little was known save its name. Ten acres in extent, it rose upon a plateau two miles out of the town of Dorchester and five more from Ramsdale. Its mounds and terraces drew many travelers in the spring and summer. Serena, who had often mentioned it to Kitty, had promised, "We'll ride there when the weather's improved."

The last week, a thaw had set in and the snow Kitty had viewed a month previously from the coach bearing them to Ramsdale was melted and most of the mud hardened on the roads. These were now dry enough to bear all manner of traffic. Kitty, riding in the direction of Maiden Castle, had passed coaches, drays, gigs and heavily-laden farm wagons, reaping a harvest of curious, and she had no doubt, disapproving stares. She had not minded them—it was only now, standing at the edge of the bare and undulating successions of terraces and roadways which she must agree, looked nothing like a castle, that she wished she had brought a groom with her. He would not have let her ride back and forth about the mound until her horse was so sadly lathered that she doubted he had the strength to bear her back to Ramsdale. He would not have let her linger until the sun lay all too low upon the western horizon. He would have been watchful where she, rapt in melancholy, was not.

"I have been foolish," she murmured as she watched the shadows settle beneath the terraces of the mound, changing narrow lanes into seeming gorges. She *had* been very foolish, and her folly was of the sort which had brought her out upon Captain Fowler's roof without informing anyone of her intentions. She had merely told the groom who had saddled Ali-Bey, the mettlesome little chestnut she had been given to ride, "I shall be in the park, and will return soon."

She had had no intention of remaining in the park. She had wanted to be away from Ramsdale and from all who dwelt within that mansion. That which she had feared had come to pass, but in a way she had not anticipated. Ever since the first visit of David Vennor, which had been followed by several more, she had expected to be informed that the Honorable Dillian would soon be returning to the bosom of her family—or, at least to the estate, her family's bosom being abroad. However, no such news had reached her, until at breakfast this morning. Gareth, who, had been on his feet since the latter days of January, had announced abruptly that they would be going to London within three days.

"To London?" Serena had stared at him anxiously. "Are you strong enough?"

His glance had been cold, his answer short. "Quite strong enough, my dear."

Though he was still pale and far too thin, Serena had not argued with him, nor had Kitty. Months ago—or had it been years?—he had told her, "I am not overfond of London. I hope you will not repine if we remain in the country much of the year?"

She had been quick to assure him that she, raised at The Oaks, could not abide the crowds, the noise, the busy thoroughfares of such cities as New Orleans, Boston, or New York. She had had no answer for him when he had said with one of the chill smiles she had learned to expect from him, "I think you must find it sadly wearisome here, Katherine. Certainly there will be more entertainment to be found in London."

"Indeed, dear Kitty, you will enjoy London," Serena had added quickly and with an affectionate glance. "I shall see that you have a proper introduction to our city."

Thinking on that exchange, Kitty shook her head slightly. When she had first met Serena, she had feared the girl, siding with her brother and with her dear friend Dillian Vennor, must harbor only resentment for her. Indeed, on the day of David Vennor's initial visit, she had thought her suspicions confirmed—as Serena must have excitedly confided the news that Dillian remained Gareth's one love.

However, much to her surprise, Serena had actually warmed to her and, not a week after her arrival, had come to her chamber to say with a bluntness she had discovered was characteristic, "You must know, Katherine, that when Gareth first informed me of his marriage, I was much disappointed, and I might add to my discredit, determined to dislike you. Dillian has always been my great and best friend. I love her, and I'll not scruple to tell you that I feared you must be a scheming adventuress. Now I see that I was quite mistaken. So I pray you'll overlook any coldness I might have shown you I want to be your friend. I only hope my brother will soon come to his senses."

In spite of these forthright words, Kitty had remained a little wary of her. It had occurred to her that Serena might merely be sorry for her—but Serena had gone out of her way to prove that she had meant it. She had seen that Kitty was given a horse to ride, and she had taken her to Dorchester and introduced her to Mrs. Bolton, a very skillful mantua-maker. Kitty glanced down at her riding habit: of dark green pelisse cloth, it was a product of that needle and a faithful copy of one she had admired in the pages of *La Belle Assemblée*. She had other new gowns at Ramsdale: a walking dress in Nile-green washing silk and a morning gown in a green and white chintz. Serena had applauded Kitty's choices; and Gareth, too, had pronounced them to his taste, but in a manner so restrained that Serena had chided, "I do not believe you realize what a beautiful wife you have, my dear."

Kitty winced. Not for the first time, she wished that Serena had refrained from an observation which, though certainly well-meant, could only have pained him. She was sure that it had, from the roughened tone in which he had obediently responded, "I must agree."

There were times when she almost hated him, not because he had been cool to her but because, seeing him each day, she was reminded of that happiness they had shared so briefly. Their situation was rendered the more miserable because of his valiant efforts to draw her out and to establish some manner of rapport with her. Though she could attribute these partially to his intrinsic kindness, she guessed they must also be part of a desperate need to understand what there was about her that had made him betray the woman he had loved all of his life.

In pursuing this course, he had taken her through the house, describing the various architectural additions, telling her anecdotes about those ancestors whose portraits hung in the Long Gallery, and later, when he felt better, he accompanied her to Dorchester and showed her St. Peter's Church, saying with a certain pride that it was the only house of worship to survive a disastrous fire in 1613. He had also pointed out an innocuous dwelling on West Street where Judge Jeffreys had held the infamous "Bloody Assizes" during which he had ordered the execution of two hundred ninety-two men for their part in the Duke of Monmouth's short-lived rebellion.

Gareth had described this event with anger—almost as if it were yet over a century ago and the heads of the traitors still affixed to poles in the nearby square.

The presence of the past seemed to be everywhere; people in the village talked about the fire of 1613 as if they could yet hear the wails of those hapless souls trapped in the burning houses. That had intrigued her until she thought of Gareth's past, which must also be cruelly present as he gazed on the streets he had walked with Dillian Vennor. To do him justice, he did make a worthy attempt to be pleasant, even husbandly, but it seemed to her that each time he looked at her the anguished questions returned to plague him.

Once, passing the library door, she had heard him conversing with Serena and suddenly he had cried out,

"Madness." She had fled, not wanting to eavesdrop, but she was sure he had been referring to that madness which had joined him to this stranger he could not love. He had asked her of her home in Virginia and inquired whether or not she would like to return for a visit now that hostilities were at an end.

The thought of such a visit had been so horrifying that she had been unable to refrain from telling him about her stepfather and his brother. While he had sympathized, he had not mentioned his own experiences with his late stepmother, and she felt that he had been sadly disappointed to learn that she could not go home. In fact, she had an uneasy feeling that he might have suggested an annulment, were it not for her dependence upon him. Once more the doctor's words concerning his condition came back to her and with them, her own frightened query about its duration.

"Could it be never?"

Despite the physician's disclaimer, it seemed very likely that it could. She had watched Gareth as closely as she might but there had not been the slightest indication of his awakening memory.

She stared out across the desolate tract of land. Though it was not far from Dorchester, the great mound, topped by winter-yellowed shrubbery, seemed to grow larger as the sky dimmed. Though she knew she must turn back, and quickly, she had difficulty tearing her gaze away from it. Serena had told her that it was regarded with awe and even terror by some of the villagers. "And though much of it is arable land, there's no one who's ever wanted to plow it. One of my nurses told me that at nightfall the old ones who lie buried in it rise from their graves and walk along the ridges until cockcrow sends them back." Serena had laughed. "I used to scream with fright and Gareth would come in and hold my hand though I think he was frightened, too."

Gareth. It had been to escape him that she had ridden this long way—but of course, she could not. If she could live separately from him, then his presence might be exorcised. He would want that, but she did not. The fact that he had wed her, even though he had been betrothed to Dillian Vennor and he had come to love her under those same circumstances, still remained in her consciousness and in spite of all indications to the contrary, she dared to hope that if his memory came back it might be as it had been before.

A windy snuffle from her mount roused her from her thoughts again. She looked about her nervously. It had grown darker and she must turn back. If she could not ride the animal as far as Ramsdale, she must reach Dorchester and find a hackney that could take her there. She eyed the horse concernedly and patting its neck found it wet to her touch. "Poor old Ali-Bey," she murmured apologetically. "I did not mean to ride you half so hard."

He was tired but surely not strong enough to bear her two miles. Winding his reins about her hand, she pulled him toward a stone; but as she stepped upon it, ready to mount, a bird flew up almost in front of them and went shrieking toward the sky while Ali-Bey reared up affrighted, his reins slipping from Kitty's hands; he galloped off, disappearing down an incline.

For a moment, she was too shocked to do anything save stand and stare in the direction he had gone. Then her rueful laughter bubbled out. The "consequences" had attacked her once again, or should she call them "the price"? Wellington Abbott had employed both terms in describing the impulsive behavior which he had so often decried and for which she had suffered "the conse-

quences" and paid "the price," more than once at The
Oaks, and of course, on Captain Fowler's roof. Yet each
time her actions had appeared perfectly understandable,
at least to herself. She could not think of such matters
now; she must needs start back to the village before it
became any darker. She could easily lose her way, if she
did not hurry. She cast a pained look at her boots; they
were tight, which had not mattered on horseback but on
foot . . . she could not think of that, either. Though she
could not see Dorchester from where she stood, she was
sure it lay in the direction in which Ali-Bey had disappeared.

She started up the incline and stopped. "Blast and
damnation," she muttered in the manner of First Mate
Briggs; the ground was softer than she had thought. The
walk would not be easy. Looking back over her shoulder
at the sun, she tensed. In only a matter of minutes, the
great globe had shed its blinding rays. Deepened in hue,
only part of it was visible. Night was coming on more
swiftly than she had thought it would and a rising wind
was chill against her face. However, she had finally
reached the top of the rise where there ought to be the
village lights to guide her—but the distance held nothing
but the undulating ridges of the mound. She frowned
—her sense of direction was generally excellent, as she
had always been able to find her way back to The Oaks,
even through some of the impenetrable woods at home;
but with a quick indrawing of breath, she recalled that
she was used to those woods. Here . . . but she had been
so sure! She turned in another direction. Again her view
was blocked by the earthen ramparts and their tufted
grasses. Perhaps she had been mistaken about the direction Ali-Bey had fled. She looked about for hoof-marks
but could not see them in the soft sliding earth. Resolutely, she started up another incline.

The moon had risen and was now well up in the sky. It was the color of fresh snow, surrounded by stars that sparkled with an icy radiance. Kitty shivered for neither her habit nor her coat were proof against the biting winds that swirled her loosened hair about her face and froze her tears before they could trickle down her cheeks. She had turned in so many directions and not once had she been able to discern the lights of the village. It was impossible not to entertain the thought that when the sun rose again, she would have joined the ghostly company said to prowl upon the mound.

At her next step, she tripped and fell. She had fallen often in her frenzied efforts to find her way, but this time, instead of rising, she crawled up yet another acclivity. She was weary, her limbs were aching, she needed to rest. Clutching her knees against her chest for warmth, she sat there taking long sobbing breaths, and against her will, remembering once more, her ordeal on the roof. In her mind's eye, she saw the leaping fires, the soldiers, and the tall young officer, the light shining on his epaulettes—later in the night, those golden fringes had been sharp against her cheek as she slumbered in his arms.

She tensed. The stretch of darkness which spread before her was invaded by a tiny point of light, so small, it seemed as though one of the stars had fallen. It was bobbing up and down in the middle of the air but rather than star-colored it was a deeper, yellower hue. For a moment she wondered if it might not be a marshlight— but she was not in a marsh. As it came closer, she saw that it was a lantern held in the hand of a solitary rider. She rose. Slipping and sliding, she descended the slope, crying out loudly, "Help, Help me, I pray you!"

She had the feeling that as her cries left her throat, the icy air must freeze them and shatter them to bits before they reached whoever was riding. And would he be afraid to approach her—would he imagine her to be one of the spectres that abided in the "castle"?

The light was coming nearer. He had heard her, he *must* have heard her—or was he veering off? "Help me, I pray you!" she called again.

"Kitty!" his voice faint and still far away, reached her. "Stay where you are, but keep calling that I might ascertain your location."

She obeyed, crying out until her throat ached. She called as she had that night in Washington . . . and then he was closer, at the foot of the mound and she, coming toward him, heard the labored breathing of his horse and smelled its acrid odor.

"Oh, God, Kitty!" He dismounted. "I was afraid I'd not find you." He put his arms around her and held her against him for a moment before he lifted her to his saddle and sprang up behind her. "Lord, Lord, you are half frozen," he exclaimed, and put part of his cloak about her.

She lay against his chest, shivering, and at that moment, quite unable to ask how it was that David Vennor had come searching for her.

The explanation came later when a for once-concerned Mary had undressed, bathed, and helped her into her nightdress and thence to a bed warmed with hot bricks. Between sips of milk laced with brandy, Kitty listened to Serena saying, "And then when the gatekeeper saw Ali-Bey come racing past him, we knew you'd ridden farther than the park. And I recalled that I had mentioned Maiden Castle. I thought it well to investigate . . . Oh, Kitty, whatever prompted you to ride so far alone?"

" 'Twas only seven miles," she replied defensively. "And I thought I should have no difficulty finding my way."

"That was very foolish. More experienced travelers than you have lost their direction in these parts. Lord, you might been frozen to death!"

"I expected that I must." She clutched the covers, glad of their woolly warmth.

Eventually, Serena kissed her good-night and left. However, just as Kitty was about to drift off to sleep, Gareth entered and came to stand at the foot of her bed, his face illumined by the leaping firelight. Why must she remember Washington again?

He stared at her in a puzzled way. "We were all most alarmed. Surely you knew you should not have gone off without warning us of your intent, Katherine."

"I know, but I thought—" she began.

"On the contrary," he interrupted reprovingly, "I cannot believe you thought at all. But no matter, I'll not refine upon it now." Moving closer to her, he took her hand, kindly adding, "I am only pleased that you are safe and sound. I'll bid you good-night, now. Sleep well, Katherine."

He left the room, taking with him any hope of sleep, as she stared after him, shivering, not with the cold but because of what he had said. Save for his slight reprimand, he might have been addressing any stranded traveler who had found shelter beneath his roof.

Later, much later, when the fire was but a mass of glowing embers and she finally at the brink of sleep, she remembered that it was David Vennor who had rescued her. There was irony in that. What would Dillian Vennor say when she learned of it—and Gareth—might he not have preferred it if she had been left to die?

The house which Serena had described to Kitty as Ramsdale's London "wing" stood in Berkeley Square and had been purchased from the family of the Earl of Alford in 1780. It was larger than many on its street, and unlike most, had a big garden. This, Serena had told Kitty, was a blessing in summer for the sweet scent of the roses and other blossoms helped combat odors from the sewers and the nearby stables.

It rose up four stories, and in addition to a large saloon and drawing room on the first floor, there was a well-stocked library; there was a smaller parlor on the second floor, and three bedrooms. There were other bedrooms and a nursery on the third floor; the fourth floor was occupied by the servants.

"I am sure Gareth must have told you that my stepmother was a famous hostess. During her tenure, I believe there must have been at least one rout every week and a ball a month, not to mention banquets! Of course, all that ended with her death. Until last year, I was still in the schoolroom and with Gareth being away . . . However, once he recovers, all that will change, I am sure. Meanwhile, my dear Kitty, you needn't fear that you will have to live like a nun. I have appointed myself your guide and shall make sure that you enjoy yourself accordingly." Serena gave Kitty a roguish smile. "It will be pleasant for us both because, since you are a married lady, I need not employ a companion. I had one with me last season, a most depressing creature, a distant cousin, fallen upon evil days, as she was forever telling me in great detail. I wrote to her last month, pensioning her off . . . oh, I can hardly wait to take you about. I am quite determined that you will become the rage—and though I can see that you are a bit daunted by London, I can assure you that your opinion must soon change and you will become its partisan because *everything* is here."

Kitty smiled and refrained from telling Serena that she had not only been daunted but extremely disappointed by a city her father had praised most highly in letters which she had read often since they were first penned.

He had come to London in 1801, as an unofficial envoy for President Jefferson. He had sent back glowing descriptions of broad thoroughfares, magnificent public buildings, historical monuments and splendid houses. Of course, he had arrived at a moment of great excitement, in October, when a peace treaty had just been concluded between Britain and France and the ominous cloud of war with Napoleon supposedly lifted. He had described beautiful illuminations in the park and streets echoing to the sound of rocket fire and pistol shots in honor of this surprising accord.

That, Kitty decided, must have blinded him to the fact that the city was dark, dingy, and overlaid with soot from sea-coal fires. Nor had he described the small, narrow, noisome alleyways that lay behind the broad avenues of Pall-Mall and Piccadilly. She could not think that, for the main, the citizens were very attractive, either. Those she had seen upon the streets were scrawny and ill-favored while their speech was well-nigh unintelligible. Furthermore, she had never heard such a din as that which arose from the moment their coach had rolled into town. The air had been filled with the cursing of drivers attempting to maneuver their way through veritable forests of vehicles drawn by single mules or teams of two, four, and eight horses, beasts which under strongly-wielded whips often added anguished snorts and whinnies to the commotion. In addition to these there were the chimney sweeps, old-clothes men, scissors-grinders, pot-menders, walk-stick and umbrella-men, mop-sellers, rosemary and sweetbriar merchants, and vendors of oranges, strawberries, cranberries, milk, pies, dough for baking, lobsters, crabs, anchovies, sage, apple tarts and muffins—

all hawking their services and wares in ringing tones on sidewalks and in the streets. Add to these cries of an entirely different nature when honest citizens became the prey of the dishonest and howled indignantly, "Stop thief! Stop thief!" after the numerous cutpurses and pickpockets who prowled, indifferent to the elderly watchmen, who seldom left their boxes and took no more action in the discharge of their duties than to shake their rattles and add their quavering voices to the general hue and cry.

The city was very indifferently policed, and one of the first notes of caution Serena had sounded was her advice to Kitty to hold fast to her "ridicule"—the current slang for reticule. Slang phrases, Kitty had learned, were popular among the young bucks of the *ton,* who delighted in using terms culled from thieves' cant and from the saloons of such pugilists as Gentleman Jackson, once the champion of England. Serena had given her a few of the more popular phrases—"so that you will not be quite at a loss, my dear."

Dutifully but unenthusiastically, Kitty had written down that *glimmers* meant eyes, *ivories,* teeth; that a *shove in the mouth* or a *coffin nail* were drinks of spirits and a *clap of thunder* a not-undescriptive term for a shot of brandy, while gin could be either *blue-ruin* or *daffy,* drunk in a *shop,* which was a sobriquet for public-house.

"I am not saying that you'll need to use any of these." Her informant had smiled. "But the gentlemen are forever talking of drinking which, I am convinced, is all they do at gambling hells—and outside of them, for that matter."

Kitty could agree to that; she had seen more than one fashionably dressed young man stumbling through the crowds much the worse for strong drink.

She did have to admit, however, that the gentlemen

and ladies who resided on the square and whom she could see from the window of her bedchamber, did seem handsome but also full of self-consequence. She was fair enough to admit that her impressions might have been colored by her interior anguish. She might have been able to share some of Serena's excitement if she had not been told that the Honorable Dillian's Aunt Hester, also known as Lady Legard, owned and occupied a residence in Mount Street, which was only a few steps away from Berkeley Square. It would be only a matter of a day or two, she reasoned, before David Vennor must bring his sister to call.

Yet, less than a week after her arrival in London, Kitty's spirits, marvelously uplifted by the intelligence that Dillian Vennor and her aunt were out of town on a visit to the North, was discovering for herself the truth of Serena's statement that everything was in London. If she were not yet the city's partisan, she had certainly ceased to be its detractor. Much as she kept reminding herself that, being an American, she ought to extol the virtues of such burgeoning citadels as Boston and New York, she could not but pronounce herself more excited by the discoveries she was continually making in London.

Within three days of her arrival, she had seen and admired antiquities which had been only words and imperfect illustrations in her books at home. She had viewed the Tower of London, walked over London Bridge, visited St. Paul's Cathedral and Westminster Abbey and joined crowds of sightseers to tread the hoary stones of Hampton Court. When Gareth, wearied by the journey from Ramsdale, still remained behind, Serena assured Kitty that it was quite permissible to be squired by other gentlemen. "Once you've been here longer, I am sure you must meet with many besides David who will be eager to take you about. Indeed, my dear, I must tell you that it is considered horribly old-fashioned to be seen in company with one's husband."

Though she had believed Serena merely comforting in advancing this theory, Kitty found that it was indeed a fact. Driving with David Vennor and Kitty to Hyde Park at the fashionable hour of five, when the *ton* gathered in curricles, high-perch phaetons, landaulettes, and barouches as well as on horseback, Serena, nodding to one or another acquaintance, dropped bits of gossip into Kitty's ear. Lord Petersham, garbed in brown and driving a brown coach, was pining for a lady named Brown—not his wife, of course. Those young bucks crowding around a trio of beauties sitting in a barouche lined in pale blue satin were paying court to Harriette Wilson, her sister Fanny and a friend, Julia Johnstone, known—Serena had lowered her voice to a mere thread of sound—as "fashionable impures" which was not a description Kitty must air in society, nor was it knowledge a gently bred female should possess. As everyone knew, Harriette had started her career at a mere fifteen by becoming the *chère amie* of Lord Craven and numbered among her present conquests such prizes as the Dukes of Argyle and Wellington!

The dark little lady in the landaulette was the Princess de Lieven, the wife of the Russian ambassador and one of the seven dragons who guarded the gates of Almack's—to which Kitty would certainly have a card—while the distinguished elderly woman in the post-chaise was Lady Melbourne. Running to fat, but still attractive, her love affairs had been the scandal of the day, that day being in the 1780's, and her known lovers had been Lord Coleraine, the Duke of Bedford and the third Earl of Egremont, who was thought to be the father of her son William Lamb—and Serena's tone was again a thread and Kitty straining to hear it—Lady Melbourne, even at this advanced age, might have had Lord Byron as her lover, had she cared to run in double harness with William's giddy bride, Lady Caroline Lamb. It was said that Byron was now turned happy benedict and spending his time with his wife Annabelle Milbanke, stupid female, who thought herself a bluestocking but was not witty enough to warrant that description—Serena, for one, did not give the marriage another three months!

Though Kitty laughed at Serena's tales, the thought of these fashionable marriages depressed her. To dwell upon them was to wonder how such hole-in-the-corner romances could be considered preferable to lying peacefully beside your wedded mate and to have his arms fast about you so that the beating of his heart stilled even the thunder of the distant cannons. These memories, coming at odd times, reactivated hopes that had been well-nigh dead when they had arrived in the city. With Dillian Vennor in the North, was it not possible that Gareth, faced with the old friends who were leaving their cards, might not feel a stirring of memory and one day, when she least expected it, look up gladly at her entrance and call her Kitty instead of Katherine?

She never let herself dwell too long upon the images that accompanied these hopes, but, perhaps, if she were to make herself the "rage" as Serena had suggested, she might excite her husband's admiration . . . he might even fall in love with her all over again! Certainly, there had been many gallants who had coveted the hand of Kitty Maynard—and not all of them from Fairfax County or Washington City. There had been the young French attaché she had met at one of Dolley Madison's levées and the stodgy but eminently eligible congressman from New York, and Robert, too. However, it was a dead bore to concentrate on her past conquests—best to concentrate on replenishing her wardrobe!

Though the mantua-maker in Dorchester had been

clever, Kitty had seen gowns in London that had fairly made her mouth water; but in view of her circumstances, she was loath to let Gareth pay for these creations. However, a chance mention of the Bank of London had put her in mind of her father's letters. In one of them, he had mentioned a transaction through which he had been able to obtain funds from his own bank in Washington to supplement those he had brought for a stay lasting three months longer than he had expected it would.

The monies he had left for Kitty's use were in that same bank and one morning, she took Mary, and with a vague tale about going to a circulating library, she signaled a hackney telling a surprised cabby to drive her to the city, proper, which lay in Westminster. Here she found the bank and produced other surprises for Mr. Sheffield, its pompous manager, obviously not used to dealing with a youthful member of the *ton,* who waxed extremely business-like when discussing accounts, trusts, transfers, and drafts. She left the bank considerably easier in her mind, since Mr. Sheffield, looking at her with some respect, assured her that, depending upon the vagaries of the mail boats, she might expect her funds within three months—four at the most, depending upon the winds. It was, he explained, forty days from Liverpool to New York and twenty-three returning, though of course, overland travel needs must be taken into account as well.

With such promises, it was safe to embark upon another "voyage," and a delightful adventure it proved to be. With Serena as her willing guide, she visited more shops than she had ever dreamed could exist—even in a city the size of London. They were on Oxford Road, Pall Mall, and in Soho—and to see the wares they displayed was to be Eve in an apple orchard! In the booths that lined Oxford Road, she was dazzled by shops specializing solely in fans—fashioned of carved ivory, of spangled crepe, and painted papers. Swansdown tippets beckoned from another shop and there were French silk shawls, dainty lace fichus, net handkerchiefs for the hair, lace or satin caps, French ruffs, kid gloves, embroidered slippers, beaded reticules, an endless array of other trifles. Jewelers displayed carnelian necklaces carved with Grecian figures and backed with gold—there were jades from China, emeralds from India, plain gold bangles, and a most beautiful snake which coiled up the arm and ended in a flat head with emerald eyes and a ruby tongue. There were marvelous stuffs on sale at an emporium called Hadley, Howell and Company, where one might also buy everything from porcelain clocks to the Circassian Corset, which gave shape to the shapeless without the stiff thrust of whalebone.

Kitty, confronted by such materials as green-and-white plaid silk, by crêpes embroided in silver, by cambric, double-sided French silks, Irish poplins, sarsenet veiling and satin cloth, by silken floss, fast replacing ribbons as a trimming, by artificial flowers and sparkling diamanté, was bedazzled. Urged to buy anything she fancied, she recalled her transaction with Mr. Sheffield and happily did as she was told. The following fortnight, she spent in having these materials fashioned into gowns which Serena and Mary pronounced ravishing.

It was not only Kitty's wardrobe that underwent additions and transformations. In eight months, her russet locks had grown long enough to be pronounced sadly out of shape by the knowing Serena. Much to Kitty's delight, she discovered that Mary, whom she had grown to like, possessed fingers even more deft than those of her much-lamented Becky Lou. Once a knowledgeable and fashionable hairdresser named Monsieur Henri had been summoned to style Milady's curls, Mary was able to follow the instructions of this august individual to admirable effect.

"I vow, I am quite envious of you. Not only is your hair of a most beautiful and unusual color, but since it curls naturally, you need not suffer paper twists as I do. And Lord Byron, as well," Serena giggled, explaining that it was common knowledge that this Apollo among poets slept with his locks in curl papers or submitted to the ministrations of a valet armed with a curling iron.

The name Byron was much on the lips of the *ton*. Being of it, he was much praised and constantly quoted, even by ladies, who pronounced themselves scandalized by his reputation. The *on-dit* about his affection for his half-sister Augusta Leigh was enough to raise eyebrows and lower voices. Kitty, however, being a stranger to London, did not rejoice in the gossip which she found was one of the chief amusements of the ladies to whom she was introduced, especially after she learned that she herself was an object of much speculation.

Indeed, when the invitations Serena had mentioned, began to arrive, Kitty, responding to some of these, found that certain conversations stopped in mid-sentence immediately upon her entering the room. Judging from the surprise with which she was greeted in some fashionable houses, she was reasonably sure that her hosts had expected her to arrive with feathers in her hair, warpaint on her cheeks, or to commit some glaring solecism which must mark her as the savage they hoped she would be. However, after her first month in the city, she noted that she was no longer treated to the astonishingly rude stares with which ladies of quality had been wont to regard her. Everyone, Serena had explained, was happily surprised, if a trifle disappointed, to find that her brother's American bride had not turned out to be a nine-days' wonder such as the Esquimaux, who had recently astounded Londoners visiting St. Bartholomew Fair.

"In fact, my love, you are a success," was the pronouncement of her sister-in-law as she stepped into Kitty's bedchamber one morning, waving a piece of vellum. "And in case you are inclined to doubt me, though I do not see how you could, considering that already you have been given a card to Almack's, here is the ultimate proof! It is an invitation to Carlton House; the three of us are to attend the Regent's ball and supper on Thursday week."

"Really!" Kitty exclaimed.

"Honest and truly! And I must add that you are singularly favored—not because of the invitation, but because as it is early March and the weather cool, you'll not be suffocated. Carlton House can be abominably hot—the Prince has a positive mania for warmth. Indeed, five years ago when he gave a ball to celebrate the beginning of his Regency, women fainted in the grand salon. However, this function will not be so elaborate, nor will there be so much of a crush."

"And no fish swimming down the center of the banqueting tables?" Kitty laughed.

"Ah, you heard of that in America?"

"Papa subscribed to *The Gentleman's Magazine*—it had an account of those festivities. It spoke of how the rooms were transformed into a garden—with roses springing out of the marble floors—I could scarcely credit it."

"You may—the Prince is very fond of show. And of pretty women. I am in hopes that this ball will mark the beginning of your career."

"My career?"

"If the Prince should dance with you, your reputation as a Queen of Society would be made. And he very well might. You are not unknown in London, you've made a very good impression on our friends, which I am sure is one reason for the invitation. I said as much to Gareth and he agreed. He is delighted with your success."

"He is!?" Kitty exclaimed.

"Certainly—it cannot but add to his consequence that you are so soon accepted by the *ton*. I know you are unhappy about his seeming indifference but I must tell you that he has listened with great interest to my accounts of your progress. He has said that were he in better health, he would give a ball himself, for he is sure that you must be a notable hostess."

"Oh . . ." Kitty breathed. "He said that?"

"He certainly did." Serena's eyes danced. "I am surprised he did not say as much to you."

"I . . . am not in his confidence." Kitty flushed.

"That will change, my dear." Serena looked at her sympathetically. "You must have patience and I might add, I think you've acted very wisely."

"Wisely?" She seemed confused.

"In not remaining in his pocket. The fact that you do not depend upon him to escort you to balls and routs and come instead with David and myself—or with Sir Alwin Parr or Lord Balcarres—can only intrigue him. I know it does. The other day, he asked me very particularly if there were any gentleman who seemed to enjoy your favors above another."

"I hope you told him that there was not," Kitty cried.

"Of course, I told him the truth—but it *has* seemed to me that Sir Alwin has been showing you marked attention. It might be to your interest to give him a little more encouragement."

"A little more encouragement!" Kitty repeated. "I find him a dead bore."

"Well, there are others. Lord Balcarres is a trifle elderly but Mr. Paunceforte is quite unexceptionable."

"I have no interest in any save my husband—and as for my seeming indifference, I suit my actions to his. I know his mind, you see!"

"I think you do not. And I might tell you that if Dillian had not played fast and loose with him—"

"Come, you are funning me," Kitty protested. "I know their love began in childhood."

"Of a truth, he had a fondness for her and for many other maidens, too—of high and low degree. 'Twas only when she proved elusive that he began to pursue her."

"He did not seem that way when we first met."

"Ah, but that was an unusual situation, was it not? War changes a man's character—for the nonce, or at least I have been told so. Later . . . he was ill and dependent upon you. If you were wise, Kitty, you'd do as I suggest and see how he takes it." Serena winked at her and moved toward the door, adding, "Come, if we're to ride in the park this morning, you must dress."

Serena left Kitty full of questions. Was she to be deliberately provocative? And was Gareth actually pleased at her success? He had given no indication of it to her—but he had asked Serena if she favored any gentleman above another? That did seem to indicate a lurking . . . dared she term it *jealousy?*

She could hardly believe that. The few times that he had accompanied her to routs and assemblies, he had quickly absented himself and gone to the cardroom. She could not blame him for that; he was subject to headaches and to stand in a room so crowded that the furniture must be taken away to accommodate the guests was sadly confining. It was not to her taste at all. It was hard to talk and just as hard to listen; and even when she did listen, she could never remember much of what had been said even by those Serena praised as notable wits. Wit, in those circles, seemed to revolve around the delicate shredding of a reputation, and reminded her of those clever caricatures prominently displayed in print-shop windows. The Regent was often the target of these cruel cartoons and much was made of his bulk; another favorite subject was his eccentric and unhappy wife, the Princess Caroline of Brunswick, over whose fate Serena had laughed. "The most dreadful woman, my dear, quite mad, 'tis said. One can only feel sorry for the Regent, even if he did marry her because of the settlements. He had much better stayed with Maria Fitzherbert, Roman Catholic or not. After all, kings used to marry commoners, look at Henry the VIII."

Kitty's mind veered away from the Regent's marital problems to her own—would Gareth really be intrigued if she flirted with the men who pursued her? None Serena had mentioned was to her fancy—Serena had not, she noticed, spoken of David Vennor, who also pursued her, albeit in a most elliptical way.

David Vennor was a different matter: Kitty liked him. She had always found him amusing, in spite of her initial encounter with him at Ramsdale. Yet she was still not quite comfortable with him. There was always the memory of the night he had found her at Maiden Castle. It had seemed to establish an intimacy between them that kept recurring at odd moments, in little chancy touches as they sat together in a post-chaise or when they danced. Serena was very fond of David Vennor, and that made the situation all the more awkward.

How lovely it would have been if Gareth had not lost his memory! But he had, and Kitty was granted no place in the remaining fragments; they were the possession of Dillian Vennor. Why was she so long away? Was it because Gareth had returned to London?

Far from being pleased at her absence, Kitty was beginning to find it oppressive. If she and Gareth were to meet . . . But there was no good thinking of that. *That* being the possibility that Dillian's passion might have cooled. In lieu of any other course, it seemed expedient to act upon the advice of her best—and possibly her only— friend in London, Serena Quentin.

Seven

"Oh, Milady," Mary breathed, admiration widening her usually narrow eyes.

Kitty pivoted in front of the long Sheraton mirror and gave her a forced smile. As the hour of nine approached, she was beginning to feel distinctly nervous. Part of her condition could be traced to the occasion but the remainder resulted from her choice of attire. A good many ladies, she knew, would be clad in white, it being the preferred hue for evening. For the eleventh time in as many minutes, she wondered if she had been wise to purchase the Parisian creation brought to her attention by Madame Maurice. One of the more esteemed mantuamakers in the city, Madame had said with apparent sincerity, "I cannot believe that there is any lady in all London who'd look so elegant in this gown."

Confronted by a satin garment designed along vaguely Greek lines and of an amber shade, enlivened by a trim of dark green leaves at sleeve and hem, colors flattering to her hair and eyes, Kitty had yielded to temptation. She had intended to wear an amber necklace and ear-drops, but Serena on seeing the gown, had insisted on bringing her mother's emeralds from the bank vault. Glittering on Kitty's ears, encircling her white throat and wound through her hair, they provided just the touch that was needed.

Kitty regarded herself in the glass and thought she looked tolerably well—but suppose Gareth did not approve the ensemble? And would he be pleased to find her wearing jewels he might have hoped to present to Dillian Vennor? She tossed her head. She was not going to let that ghost haunt her this night! Taking up her wrap, another new and delightful confection, fashioned from the hair of the female llama and sewn at shoulder and hood with Britannia trimming, which Madame Maurice had assured her was far more esteemed than fur this season, she smiled a good-night to Mary, emerged from her chamber, and started down the stairs. As she reached the first landing, she came to a stop—Gareth, with Serena at his side, was in the hall below, smiling up at her, quite as if he knew her to be . . . Kitty?

Clutching the balustrade, she stared at him, her heart pounding heavily. Could he have possibly recovered his senses? Certainly he looked much like the handsome young soldier she had met all those months ago. Of course, some of that could be attributed to his attire: his black evening suit became him as much as his uniform had. There was a fall of fine lace at his throat, and beneath his jacket she caught the gleam of a silver-embroidered brocade waistcoat. There were silver buckles on his shoes and again she was aware of slim ankles and a leg which needed none of the careful padding certain less well-favored gentlemen used to fill out their stockings. A jeweled court sword was at his side and a *chapeau bras* beneath his arm.

Serena, at her best in a white silk gown trimmed with blue ribbons to match her eyes and a chaplet of pearls in her dark hair, clutched Gareth's arm. "La, is not Kitty a picture?"

"Indeed, yes," he agreed. "I must applaud your choice, a most becoming color, my dear Katherine."

"I thank you, Sir." She came down the remaining stairs to sketch a slight curtsey. If she were disappointed, she had no intention of letting him see it, nor would she let it dull the exhilaration she was beginning to experience. Impossible not to be excited at seeing Carlton House and meeting the Regent. Caricatures notwithstanding, he was a member of the House of Hanover and soon to be King of England. Generations of Maynards had served these princes until loyalty to their new country had decreed otherwise. As one of English heritage, she could not help but feel rarely privileged.

Her mood remained elevated even though the drive to Pall Mall, the avenue on which the palace was located, was of much longer duration than usual by reason of the streets being choked with carriages all going in the same direction. Nor did she join Serena in carping over the tedious period of waiting before their coachman could maneuver their post-chaise into a courtyard, so crowded that many vehicles locked wheels making passage not only uncertain but dangerous. Finally, they descended and passing between the columns, were ushered into the Great Hall.

Though Kitty had learned via the instructive pages of *The Gentlemen's Magazine* that this apartment was forty-four feet long and twenty-nine feet high, she was surprised to find it much diminished by the number of people inside. There was hardly room to walk. She had hoped to obtain a glimpse of the bronze busts of Greek and Roman statesmen executed by the famed sculptor Joseph Nollekens, but her short stature made it impossible to catch even a gleam of metal. She was able to see the oval skylight as well as the sculptured ornaments on the vaulted ceiling. Though the sculptor's work was again represented in the adjoining vestibule, her view was restricted to a glimpse of crimson velvet draperies and of a painted ceiling centered by an immense crystal chandelier.

As she was swept along by the crowds, Kitty gave up all hope of seeing the treasures of which she had read and heard so much, and narrowed her concern to a contemplation of the gowns donned for the occasion. She was relieved to discover that, while there was a great deal of white to be seen, there were other colors as well. She was aware that, as they moved from room to room, she was receiving marked attention from various gentlemen, some of whom she recognized. Smiling cordially at everybody and at nobody, she darted a glance at Gareth, hoping that he had noticed this flattering concentration of attention. If he had, he gave no sign of it; he seemed merely to be staring blankly in front of him.

"Ah, my dear, how clever of you not to wear white!" David Vennor had stepped to Serena's side, but his eyes were fixed on Kitty. "You shine like a bird of paradise amidst a gaggle of geese."

"La," Serena said lightly, but with anger in her eyes, "how am _I_ to take that?"

"As it was intended, my dear, which was never for you, whose needs must grace any gown you put on."

"Here's gallantry, or should I call it prevarication?" Serena said, but her eyes were warm again.

Kitty hoped devoutly that David would restrain his gallantries—or his prevarications—toward her; it would not do to arouse Serena's enmity. As they moved forward, she forgot this incipient problem, for they had come in sight of the Great Staircase. Once more reality had outstripped all printed descriptions of that immense double stairs which rose against two archways, the niches of which were filled with huge bronze statues. One depicted Atlas carrying a circular map of Europe on his head, and the other was Time, similarly burdened by a large round clock. On the way upstairs, she passed the celebrated equestrian painting of George II. As she admired it, she was pleased it was not a portrait of the Third George, else her patriotic convictions must have kept her concentrating solely upon the horse.

Once, Kitty might have whispered this bit of irreverent nonsense to Gareth; the fact that she could not, dared not, momentarily closed her behind a wall of grief. She was hardly aware of descending the stairs. It was only when a cool breeze ruffled her hair that she found that they had progressed into a colonnaded vestibule which seemed to stretch for miles. It took her a moment to realize that the effect was achieved by a series of cleverly positioned mirrors between the columns and at either end of the chamber. Also between the columns were tall windows opening on a lighted lawn.

As they emerged from this apartment, Gareth surprised her by drawing her aside—but it was only to say, "Look, Katherine, this is a famous view."

She saw a succession of opened doors giving her glimpses of golden walls, of high bookshelves, of carved paneling and finally of a conservatory. Gothic in design and ornament, this final chamber seemed to be constructed mainly of glass, which she knew to be tall windows emblazoned with coats of arms of every ruler from

129

William I to George III. In the very center of this vista was the artfully lighted sculpture of a Venus, drowsing on her marble couch.

"Ah," Kitty breathed, "that must be the Canova."

"You can recognize his work even at this distance!" he exclaimed.

She laughed. "I know it only from the descriptions I've read of this palace, but the printed word is certainly a poor substitute for the reality." Excitedly, she added, "Do you suppose we might examine the statue more closely?"

"We'd best make our way to the ballroom, Katherine," he said firmly. He took her arm and guided her in that direction. Mirrors were everywhere, and as they passed them, Kitty thought that for once looking glasses lied. With his hand on her arm, Gareth appeared protective of the young woman by his side, but only she knew how stiffly he held himself, as if he were afraid of coming too near her, afraid, reluctant or—what was probably more to the point—resentful.

More mirrors were ranged around the ballroom. Great pier glasses set into the walls, they faced each other and their surfaces captured the whirling dancers, wafting them down shadowy corridors to infinity. Kitty counted no less than twelve beautiful lustres hanging from the ceiling and another counting assured her that the elaborate, gold-framed girandoles with their concave or convex surfaces reflecting their candles also numbered twelve. The chamber itself was huge enough to accomodate two orchestras playing on high platforms hung with crimson silk. Though it was an impressive sight, it was almost too overwhelming. She turned to Gareth with this observation only to find that he had disappeared. His place was quickly taken by numerous gentlemen who buzzed about her like so many gnats, demanding dances. As she inscribed their names on the spokes of her fan, she saw out of the corner of her eye that Gareth had been waylaid by a tall man in a military uniform ablaze with orders. His face looked familiar, and as she was swept away in a waltz, she recognized him as the Duke of Wellington, whose likeness had appeared in many an illustrated paper at home.

At first, Kitty was pleased to have her mind distracted by dancing. But as Serena had warned, the palace was hot and the ballroom particularly overheated, so that after she had gone through the paces of a quadrille, two country dances and several waltzes, she thought with longing about those windows that opened onto the lawn in the colonnaded vestibule. It was not until she was engaged for a waltz with David Vennor that she dared ask if he might take her there. Though he assented with gratifying speed, it appeared to Kitty that her request seemed to amuse him.

She thought she must have divined the reason when, upon entering the apartment, she found that it, too, was very warm. However, he was quick to steer her to a window which he opened, bringing in a surprisingly chill gust of wind. "Come." He put his arm around her. "You'll catch your death."

"I shan't," she said, stepping toward the aperture. "I find it marvelously refreshing. If we'd not left the ballroom, I am sure I should have swooned."

"That would have been a pity." He was close to her again. "Females are never at their best when they swoon, for they turn blue. Blue's not your color; it should be either green or gold."

She laughed. "I cannot think that a green complexion would be flattering, either."

131

"You choose to misunderstand me," he complained. "You are looking uncommonly beautiful tonight, my dear."

"I thank you, Sir." She stared up into the night sky. The stars were bright and the moon nearly full. Unwillingly, she was reminded of that night when he had rescued her. He was very close to her now. She could feel his breath on her cheek. Was he being besieged by similar memories? She feared he might be and knew, in that moment, that she had erred in asking him to take her out of the ballroom. She said, "At home, Papa had a telescope. He used to tell me the names of the constellations. I wish I could remember them."

"Why?" he asked huskily.

"Are you not interested in the configurations of the heavens?"

"I am content to fix my attention on objects near enough for me to see clearly and to touch—such as certain devilishly provocative females, who deliberately set out to torment a man . . ."

She tensed but managed a light laugh. "I should not think that they would be particularly comfortable company, Sir."

"Not comfortable, perhaps, but infinitely beguiling and enough to . . ." He paused as from the hallway a familiar voice reached them, saying in anguished tones, "That is the truth of it, Lady Powis. I cannot remember writing to you. Indeed, I am more shocked than I can say. As you know, Dick and I were close friends. I . . . I thought him still in America and had been wondering when I might hear from him again. I did not dream that he was dead. I pray you will understand my . . . infirmity."

"Poor lad, poor lad." The answer came in the hushed and saddened tones of an elderly woman. "I do understand and I pray you will forgive me. I'd not distress you for the world, but I've been from town and have lived mainly in seclusion since Richard was taken from me. I'd not heard of what befell you. Come . . . you'd best have a brandy."

"Not yet. I'd better wait until . . ." His voice broke. "I beg your pardon, Lady Powis, but would you mind if I did not escort you back? In my present . . . unmanly state, I should not add to the general merriment."

"Not unmanly, my dear Gareth, never unmanly. I shall go, and I hope you'll come to see me. I'll be in town until July."

"I shall and soon. I—I am indeed sorry for your loss. I'd not a better friend than Dick, as I think you know."

"I do and know, too, that my son prized your friendship above all others. I am glad that you were with him at the last, very glad." There was a whisper of silk and the sound of soft diminishing footsteps.

It was followed by a harsh sob: "Oh, God, dead and I not *remembering*."

"I must go to him," Kitty whispered.

"Perhaps I'd best fetch Serena," David said concernedly.

"No." She put a restraining hand on his sleeve. "It's I who can best help him. I was with him when his friend died." Moving swiftly away from him, she stepped into the corridor and saw Gareth near the doorway, his face buried in his hands. Running to him, she said urgently, "My dear . . ."

He raised his head and regarded her with tear-filled eyes. "K-Katherine . . ."

She heard resentment in his tone and knew he could not welcome her intrusion. Yet, it was to his interest that she persist. "Gareth, I heard what passed between you and Lady Powis and blame myself for your confusion.

133

You should have had that account from me—so much happened afterward that the tragedy was swept from my mind."

"You knew . . ."

"Yes and might have spared you a recurrence of your grief. I pray you'll excuse—"

"Please," he said gently, "I cannot fault you, Katherine. You could not know how I esteemed him. We went through much together . . ."

"I remember."

"And I do not. Oh, God!" He ran his hands through his hair. "Was it a cruel death, Katherine?"

"It was not as hard as you might think. Come, let's go home and I'll tell you all I know."

"You'd leave?!" he said in surprise.

She was surprised in turn. "You cannot want to remain?"

"No, I cannot, but you, my dear . . . The festivities are hardly underway and I think you've not been presented to the Regent."

"Can you believe that matters to me?"

"Nor have you partaken of supper. The suppers here are famous."

"Have you not *listened* to me?"

"I have, but can hardly credit it. I know you've looked forward to this ball. Surely David or another of your friends could escort you home."

"Let David escort your sister and let me go with you. It's only right that you hear as much as I can tell you. Wait. David's here."

"Here?"

"I was feeling dizzy from the heat and begged he'd bring me where I might breathe fresh air. Hold and I will explain to him, though there's little need. We both heard your conversation with Lady Powis." She hurried back to

134

the windows and confronted David. "I am sure you know what I mean to say. Please take Serena home."

"Of course, if that is what you wish," he replied in a low voice. "But I agree with Gareth—it would be a pity for you to hurry away so soon."

"I do not understand you," she whispered. "Can you think I could leave him unhappy and uncertain as to the fate of his friend when it's within my power to enlighten him?"

"Can you think that this . . . enlightenment will add to his happiness?"

"I know that the lack of it must increase his misery."

"I tell you, Kitty, you exert yourself for nothing. Here's a man who cannot appreciate the treasures that lie within his grasp." He put his hand on her arm.

She twisted away from him, and said only, "I pray you will take Serena home." Coming back to Gareth, she told him, "It's all arranged and I am at your disposal."

"You are very kind," he said heavily. "I cannot believe that I deserve your consideration."

She smiled up at him. "I assure you that you deserve as much as I can give."

He regarded her for a long moment. "So much must be buried in my head. I would it were possible to extract it and see it before me, as one can an ailing tooth."

"I'll do my best to provide the proper instruments."

She was rewarded by the ghost of a smile and even more by his halting: "I am pleased that you are coming with me, Katherine. Let us hurry so that we may avoid notice. It cannot be thought proper for either of us to leave so early."

As she walked back with him through those magnificent apartments, Kitty had no eye for them. Her heart was very full. It ached for this new misery he must endure for it had been hard enough to lose his friend—to suffer that loss a second time ... Thinking on it, it seemed to her that her own suffering was eclipsed. Surely, it was better to have sad memories than to possess none at all.

"And—afterward, you told me that the shell exploded so quickly that you were sure he could have felt nothing," Kitty concluded. At Gareth's request, they had come into the library; seated near him on the sofa, she stared into the fire.

"I thank you," he said after a moment's pause.

Turning toward him, she saw that his cheeks were wet. She longed to hold him against her as she had on the day he had returned to fall into her arms and lie there grieving for his friend, but she made no move. Unlike Captain Powis, she had no one to speak for her and bring her forth from those shadows that had hidden her from him. Her every instinct warned against her doing it for herself.

A log fell. Startled by the sound, she looked into the fireplace again and saw a mass of sparks fly upward. He said, "Fire ... cross fire ... trees close together ... leaves dry ... some burning ..." He paused, staring unseeingly at Kitty.

She sucked in her breath and held it, not wanting to disturb his concentration by even so small a sound as breathing. Was he remembering? *Was he?*

"And the ground burned, too ... pitted. Sharp stones ... smoke ... sound ... loud ..."

The door to the library was pushed open and Serena hurried in. "My dearest Gareth, what's this, are you ill?"

Kitty sprang to her feet. "I pray you ..." she began,

wanting to caution Serena to say no more, wanting to thrust her bodily from the room, but there was no halting her onward rush, no silencing her frantic questions.

"What's amiss, my dear? I came as soon as ever I might. The Regent had just entered and we were all bowing and I could not leave and—"

"There was no need for you to leave!" Kitty exclaimed. "I was with him."

Unheeding, Serena knelt at Gareth's side. "Oh, you do look pale . . . I was so sorry when David told me what had happened. Do you have another headache, love?"

"No, I thought . . . just for a moment . . . I thought that I . . ."

"Remembered!" Kitty cried. "You *did* remember something! Oh, Gareth, think . . . think and we'll all be quiet. Perhaps there's more that will come."

He regarded her uncertainly. "I thought . . . but, no, it's gone. 'Twas but a flash of something . . ."

"Fire, cross fire, trees, the ground pitted, smoke," she prompted. "Concentrate, Gareth, I beg you—concentrate!"

"Kitty!" Serena spoke with unaccustomed sharpness. "Pray desist. You are confusing him. Can you not see that you are?"

An equally sharp retort sprang to Kitty's lips. Resolutely, she downed it. It was too late for reprimands or protests. At that moment, however, she was perilously close to hating Serena. If she had not come bursting into the library—if she had not come at all . . . There was no *need* for her to come. She had told David as much—why had he been impelled to bring her home? Kitty's native common sense intervened to tell her that she was not being fair. Serena was concerned for her brother. She could have had no inkling of the harm her ill-timed interruption had wrought. Still, Kitty could have wept with disappointment. If he had been left alone, he might have remembered everything about that day and more besides. She said stiffly, "I am sorry."

"Please," Gareth protested. "You need proffer no apologies, Katherine. You were kind to come with me."

"Uncommonly kind!" Serena exclaimed. "But you need not have left the ball, Kitty dear. You could have waited. There were many long faces when it was learned you'd departed. If you'd told me Gareth was not well, I should have returned with him and gladly."

"There was no need for either of you to have returned." Gareth's tone was impatient. "I was not ill and in truth, I did my best to dissuade Katherine, but she'd not listen."

Kitty faced him. "I told you, but it seems I must repeat myself, that I wanted to come with you."

"You are a dear girl," Serena said, "and of course you need not repine. There will be other invitations to Carlton House and much else to keep you occupied, Kitty."

"I'd not care if there were not." Kitty's annoyance was rising again. More of this conciliating chatter and the wretched girl would have Gareth believing that she actually did regret having left the stupid ball. "Indeed, it was at my suggestion—" she began, only to have Serena interrupt.

"Gareth, my dear, you are looking exhausted. Should you like to retire?"

He rose. "Yes, I think I should." He moved to Kitty and brought her hand to his lips. "I do thank you, Katherine."

"No need to thank me. I am Kitty, Kitty, Kitty, your wife and I love you," she longed to cry out. *"Oh, Gareth, my love, do remember!"* But it would be no use. The

138

moment when he might have remembered had tumbled back into oblivion, unwittingly banished by his sister. Aloud, she said, "I do wish you a good-night, Gareth," and stood smiling valiantly as he left the room.

Eight

"Milady." A gentle touch on Kitty's shoulder brought her out of what she could only describe as the tangled skein of a dream. It had gone every which way, taking her down winding corridors, presenting faces to her, some familiar, some she had never seen. She had been in many different rooms but already their physical aspects, vivid in the span of her dream, were fragmented. She recalled a painted ceiling, a marble pillar, a broken statue, a waxen effigy, a crowded floor where figures whirled, and, more recognizable, the lights on the Pavillion at Vauxhall Gardens—from which she concluded that she had been wandering through places visited with Serena, with David Vennor and with Sir Nigel Palfrey, a recent acquaintance, introduced to her by Serena, whose special friend he seemed to be.

Opening her eyes, Kitty was surprised to find her chamber full of sunlight. "What is the hour?" she murmured.

"It's a quarter past eleven, Milady. I'd not have disturbed you, but your fitting's at one."

"Past eleven!" Kitty stared at Mary incredulously. "I have never slept so long."

"You retired very late, Milady."

"Late . . . oh, yes, it was whist at Lady Ogleby's, was it not?"

"At Lady Palfrey's, I believe."

"Ah . . . Sir Nigel's aunt. These evenings have a way of blending into each other so I have trouble distinguishing one from the next. I did play with that old cheat . . ." Kitty clapped a hand over her mouth and smiled ruefully at Mary. "You must not betray me. If the word should reach Lady Palfrey's abigail and be wafted into her mistress's ear, I shall be in deep disgrace."

Though Mary's face remained impassive, there was a gleam in her eyes. "If your ladyship will forgive me, 'tis a failing so well known that it has ceased to be the subject of discussion among us. I hope you did not lose too great a sum."

"On the contrary, I won."

"You won!" Mary cried excitedly.

"Lady Palfrey practices no sleight of hand—her wines are potent and her suppers heavy. I bested her by quaffing water and nibbling at my food." Kitty bent a stern eye on Mary. "I charge you to keep that secret close." She paused as she heard a gentle tap at the door.

"That would be Miss Serena," Mary said. "She's come three times already."

"Pray admit her, then." Kitty sat up against her pillows.

Serena's first expression after her greeting was a series of complicated gestures in the direction of Mary, by which Kitty divined she was to dismiss her abigail. That having been done, her sister-in-law perched on the end of the bed. "I vow," she complained, "I thought you must sleep the morning away. Were you wearied by your victory? Lady Palfrey swears she'll never play with you again! And Sir Nigel's delighted. He says his aunt has fleeced him so often, he's lost count."

"Let him keep a clear head," Kitty returned crisply. "He'll win, too, though I doubt that would be easy for him."

"Come, you're too hard on him. He's fond of you."

"Fonder of you, though I pray you've not lost your heart to him."

"Tush, he's just a friend." Serena looked down. "I've lost my heart to no one . . . I am in no rush to wed."

Kitty heard a touch of defiance in her tone and noticed that there was a frown in her eyes; but since she had a feeling Serena would not want to be questioned on her state of mind, she said merely, "What is it that you wanted to tell me that Mary must not know?"

Serena's eyes brightened. "Something very exciting, my dear. Sir Nigel knows an opera singer—"

"Only one? I should think he would number several among his acquaintance—opera dancers, too. Is that counted exciting?"

"Will you heed me? He's obtained cards to a Masquerade at the Opera House—we'll go there directly after the play tonight."

"Oh, no," Kitty protested.

"No?" Serena's face fell. "But we've nothing afoot after the theatre and 'twill be such rare sport. I've never been to one and I should hate to miss it. You know I may not go without you."

Kitty was silent, regarding Serena curiously. In the last three weeks, it seemed to her that they had had a surfeit of what Serena considered "rare sport." They had attended assemblies and routs. They had driven to Richmond for a picnic and gone to subscription balls on Wednesday nights at Almack's and also made regular visits to the Haymarket, Drury Lane, Covent Garden, the Italian Opera and Astley's Amphitheatre, not to mention the teas and card-parties in between. For her part, she was heartily tired of her hectic existence. If she had enjoyed one or two such pleasures a week so that she might have reflected upon them at her leisure, she would have been more content. The only real excitements she could remember had occurred on the night of the Carlton House Ball, when Gareth had displayed signs of returning memory, and on the occasion he had taken Serena and herself to see Edmund Kean perform the role of Shylock in *The Merchant of Venice* at Drury Lane.

She could remember that evening with remarkable clarity, even to her disappointment when the famous tragedian had turned out to be a small and very ugly little man, whose initial appearance had sent a titter of laughter ricocheting through the audience. It was stilled long before he launched into his famous speech:

"Hath not a Jew eyes? Hath not a Jew hands, organs, dimensions, senses, affections, passions? Fed with the same food, hurt with the same weapons, subject to the same diseases, healed by the same means, warmed and cooled by the same winter and summer as a Christian is?"

The voice had been incredibly beautiful, that plea had moved the audience to tears, and Kitty with them. But despite Kean's remarkable performance, whole pas-

144

sages of it had been obliterated for her as she watched Gareth. For the time it had taken Shylock to lose his case, Gareth had been enthralled. Seemingly the burden of his destroyed memory had dropped away and he had fallen completely under the actor's spell. If it had wrung her heart to suffer the never-failing but distant courtesy with which he treated her, to hear him call her Katherine and to never penetrate the barrier that had risen between them, it was the more painful to see him animated and looking so like the man she had learned to love—yet, at the evening's end, to find him still indifferent to her.

It was very difficult to credit Serena when she insisted her brother was pleased by the *ton*'s acceptance of his wife. If he found pleasure in her social successes, in the flowers that were sent to her by various amorous gentlemen and in the interest displayed by well-known hostesses, he had very little to say on the subject— certainly very little to say to her. Any hope that his attitude might change toward her after the Carlton House Ball had been dashed when he had made his appearance the following morning—to apologize yet again for having spoiled her enjoyment of the evening. He had spoken to her as if she were a guest in his house; indeed, his whole bearing suggested that, rather than regarding her as a member of his family, he thought of her as a visitor who must in time go home.

Kitty winced. She did not like to think about what was still her only real home. She had written so often to her mother, but had heard nothing. Of course, it did take a long time for letters to cross the ocean. It would be another week before Kitty could call at the bank and obtain her funds. She grimaced. Immediately she had them in her possession, she would return all Gareth had expended on her wardrobe and which she had chafed at taking. Prices were high and the man she called husband was that in name alone—one more reason she had let Serena persuade her to the hectic gaieties of the town.

"Kitty!" Serena exclaimed impatiently. "Does it take so long to give me an answer?"

"An answer?"

"I vow, you must be half asleep again. The Masquerade . . . may we not attend?"

"Will it last the night?"

"It will end whenever you wish it to end. Though do not suppose that once you're there, you'll be in such haste to leave. Please, Kitty, say you'll come."

"Very well," she assented. "I will."

"Ah!" Serena embraced her ecstatically. "I do thank you. I should have been desolated if I'd had to refuse. But—" she lowered her voice—"I charge you, say nothing of this to Gareth?"

"He'd not approve? Perhaps we'd best not go," Kitty said quickly, glad to seize upon this excuse.

"In his present mood, Gareth might object to the company. There are no social barriers in the opera house—all manner of people attend, singers, actors, cits, that's what makes them so entertaining—but I hear everyone is very well behaved, and besides we'll be masked and escorted by Sir Nigel and David."

"Shall we wear costumes?"

"No, I shall obtain two dominoes. I can borrow them from friends of mine. I promise you, Kitty, this will be an evening you'll not forget."

"Did I not tell you it would be exciting?" Serena demanded.

Clad alike in black dominoes and matching half-masks, the two girls were seated in a box above the stage. They had arrived at the opera house some twenty minutes earlier, and at Sir Nigel's suggestion had sought out this eyrie. " 'Tis best we should be spectators rather than participants," he had said. "At least at first."

Kitty, who would not have credited him with such good sense, was in agreement. She had been dismayed by the clamor that had greeted them as they had entered. In fact, she had no desire to become part of the rowdy festivities on the stage. The immense auditorium had been stripped of its seats and bands positioned at various points upon it and on the stage as well. These bodies, rather than playing in unison, struck up the music for quadrilles, waltzes, and country dances. Oddly enough, those going through the paces of these dances seemed to have no trouble suiting their steps to the individual rhythms. The overall effect was, she thought, singularly strident and unnerving.

Equally unnerving were the activities of some of the pirates, harlequins, columbines, clowns, Turks, Orange-girls, Circassian slave-girls, monks, nuns, and those who like themselves preferred the simpler disguise of dominoes and masks, strolling around the hall or congregating in its darker corners. A goodly number of them seemed to be badly foxed and certainly there was a disproportionate amount of embracing and fondling as certain bold gentle-men pressed their attentions on some very acquiescent females. Kitty's regret at allowing Serena to persuade her into attending an entertainment which showed every sign of becoming more rather than less boisterous increased. There would be a supper served later, Serena had told her, but Kitty had no desire to attend. The music, the giggles, screams and shouts were beating against her ears; her head was aching and her only desire was to leave as soon as possible.

"Well, why not?" Serena said angrily.

Startled, Kitty swung around to find her glaring down at David. He merely smiled. "Because I choose to watch, my dear."

"You mean you choose to . . ." Serena caught Kitty's gaze and frowned at her. Tossing her head, she turned to Sir Nigel. "Will *you?*"

He rose. "Of course, at your service, ma'am."

"Come, then." Serena moved toward the door of the box.

"Where are you going?" Kitty asked.

"I wish to dance." Serena's tone was curiously chill. "Sir Nigel will partner me, since David appears to be afraid."

David's eyes glinted with laughter through the slits of his mask. "I am not afraid," he drawled. "I am just not . . . in the mood."

"Serena." Kitty rose. "I pray you'll not go down there. Those are not at all the sort of people with whom you should rub shoulders."

"I pray *you'll* not be a spoilsport!" Serena retorted. "I came here to enjoy myself and enjoy myself I shall. Sir Nigel will protect me, will you not?"

"Of a truth, I shall. Glad to do it . . . Y' needn't worry about her, Lady Quentin." He smiled at Kitty. He was a tall, fair youth with what she considered a foolish grin. He had little in the way of conversation but he was powerfully built and was known to have gone several rounds with Gentleman Jackson without much hurt from the champion's punishing fists. Still Kitty could not approve Serena's joining the crowds below.

"Please, I beg you . . ." she began and stopped for the pair had left the box. Intending to follow them, she started forward, only to have David pull her down.

"She'll take no harm."

"But—"

"I tell you, Nigel's uncommon handy with his fives. He'll floor any bumpkin who dares approach her."

"I never should have let her persuade me into coming here. If I'd known what manner of—entertainment it was, I would have refused. I cannot think what Gareth would say were he to find out—which I hope he does not."

"Gareth has other matters on his mind, my dear." David moved his chair closer to hers. "My sister's coming home."

"Your sister? When?"

"On the morrow. Did not Serena tell you?"

"No, she did not," Kitty said through stiff lips.

David stood up and held out his hand. "Come, my sweet, let's find a quieter corner. I must speak with you."

Dazed, she took his proffered hand and let him lead her out of the box and down the narrow hall behind it. She did not know where he was taking her. Her mind was picturing the inevitable meeting between Dillian and Gareth. She could not help but believe that it would have a momentous effect on her life. Once more she was thinking of that moment when he had nearly remembered. If only he had . . . but he had not, and now . . .

"Let us stop here."

She glanced around her. They had come into a sort of cul-de-sac. It was very dark. The only light reaching it was from a guttering pair of candles in a sconce some paces down the hall. "What . . ." she began and stopped, not quite sure what she wanted to say.

"Kitty, my dear love, why do you not cease to flutter your wings against this particular lustre? It would be a pity to see so lovely a moth become a cinder."

149

"I beg you'll not jest with me," she protested sharply.

"I am not jesting. I wish to speak for my sister and myself as well. You have it in your power to mend three broken hearts—four, if you count your own."

"I do not understand you."

"I speak for Gareth and for Dillian. I've not heard much from my sister since she's been away, but she and I were always very close—far closer than with anyone else in the family. I've always understood her better. I was with her when she received Gareth's letter. She said very little, but, as I say, I know her. I know it was a deathblow. Had he been here, I should have called him out; and, were it not for my friendship with Serena, I should have broken off all congress with the family. I am glad I did not because I have met you. But my poor sister . . ."

She put out her hand. "Please."

"I know I am wounding you. I wonder . . . I've often wondered what there is about this man that he can command love so easily and deserve it so little. Be that as it may, Dillian loves him and he loves her and has married you! You could release him—you could divorce him. I know you'll say that divorce is wrong, but is it so wrong under these circumstances? I know not what exactly made him marry you—and he does not remember. I know, however, that it is not love. Release him, Kitty. Give him back to Dillian and take me instead. This action will not bring disgrace upon you. If you were divorced a thousand times, I should still love you and want you. Does that surprise you? You believe me a light-hearted trifler. Do not trouble to deny it. I remember our first meeting and 'tis much to my discredit. However, I shall tell you that my heart was whole then—and is no longer. You may believe that I was the particular friend of

Serena, but I was not. Her affections are fixed on none. Kitty . . . be kind. Be kind to *all* of us—let Gareth go and come to me as my love and as my wife."

Kitty had listened in mingled fear and pain. As he concluded, she said hesitantly, for it was difficult to keep her voice steady, "I think it is early to—to discuss such matters."

"Early!" he exclaimed. "Damn you, Kitty, I have laid my heart at your feet. Do you regard it so lightly?" Before she could answer, he continued in a low, passionate voice, "It might be early, but I want you to know where I stand, where I have stood since that night at Maiden Castle when I held you in my arms. If you only knew how often I have dreamed of that ride and wished it might have continued from here to Land's End . . . Kitty—" he put his hands on her shoulders—"it is becoming harder and harder for me to be in your company and not speak and not—"

"I pray you," she said sharply, "do *not* speak." Kitty edged away from him. "I am indeed sorry if you cherish these sentiments, but I must tell you that they are in vain. They are not returned."

"Not yet, but maybe soon. Are you not weary of your shadow husband? You are too much of a woman to be content with such as he. If you do not believe my words, I have other ways of convincing you." He caught her in his arms and pressed a long kiss on her mouth.

Furiously, Kitty struggled against him, but he was too strong for her. Pushing her to the floor, he threw himself down beside her and began to drop kisses on her cheeks and throat.

She was terrified but knew it would be no use to cry out. No one would hear her and, if they did, she would be counted as coy and teasing. She had seen many couples in similar positions on the floor below. The only tactic open to her was to lie passive and accept his caresses until he relaxed his hold.

It seemed a long time before he finally raised his head to smile triumphantly and say, "What will you tell me now, my dearest? Will you not say that we were meant to love? Come, sweet liar, say me nay—with your lips yet warmed by mine!"

Kitty clenched her fist and thrust it full into his smiling mouth As his hold loosened, she leaped to her feet and fled through the corridor. He was after her in a trice but she came upon a flight of stairs and dashed down it, emerging hard by one of the platforms on which a band was grinding out a German waltz. She felt herself seized and whirled into the midst of the dancers. A scream died on her lips as she found it was not David who held her but a tall man in a pirate's costume, who laughed drunkenly and danced around and around until he fell at her feet, still laughing. Dizzy and half-sobbing, she staggered away from him, only to be seized by a man in monk's robes.

"Ah, 'ere's a pretty bit o'muslin. Foxed, are ye? C'mon, gi' us a look at yer face." His hot, brandy-scented breath was in her nostrils as he fumbled with the strings of her mask. A second later, he had cried out in surprise, as she thrust her crooked elbow into his stomach. She broke from him and hurried across the crowded floor, trying to evade the masked and drunken roisterers who clutched at her. Her mind was in a turmoil. She could not let David find her again: he had gone mad, but Serena— where was Serena, she could not leave without her, yet how could she search for *anyone* in this great seething mass of people? Then, ahead of her she sighted the tall form and white-blond head of Sir Nigel Palfrey. Thankfully, she hurried to his side.

"Sir Nigel, I pray you—"

"Pray? You pray, do you?" The tall masked man grinned down at her. "I'd say you were the answer to my prayers, damned if you're not, my little ladybird." He caught her arm.

"Please . . ." She endeavored to free herself. "I mistook you. You are not—"

"What does it matter who I am not? Who I *am*'s what's important and who are *you?*" His grasp tightened. "You have a pretty voice, and I'll warrant a pretty face beneath that mask." With his other hand, he thrust her hood back. "Ah, I am mighty partial to redheads. Give a man a good time, they do." He bent his head and pressed a suffocating kiss upon her lips.

Terrified, she struggled against him, but her strength was unequal to his hard embrace. She felt his fingers fumbling at the strings of her mask. Wrenching it off, he drew in his breath. "Zounds, it's a little beauty, a prime article if I ever saw one." He slipped his hand inside her cloak and tore at her bodice. "Let's make this unmasking complete, my sweet love."

She could not keep from screaming and screaming again. A young man suddenly stepped forward. "What's this? Why are you forcing your attentions on this lady?"

"What do you mean, forcing my attentions?" her captor snarled. "I paid for 'em, paid well, I did. If you do not believe me, ask that old harpy over there—" He jerked a hand over his shoulder—"Mother Biddle, who sold her to me for the evening, and a pretty price she asked, too."

" 'Tis a lie," Kitty screamed; and, seeing the man's attention was momentarily diverted, she darted away toward the side of the hall. She found a door, pushed it open and burst outside—suddenly shivering in the icy winds. She clutched her cloak about her and leaned against the wall of the building, striving to catch her breath. Loud voices reached her and she looked up to see two fashionably dressed young men lurching past.

"Where's the Charley?" one of them yelled. "Got to find us a Charley an' upset 'is box. Lay you a pony, it's me that does it this time."

"Lay you a pony, you're wrong," mumbled his friend.

"Don' think he's up this street . . . next street . . . ah, what have we here?"

The pair looked in her direction, their intention of knocking over a watchman's box evidently forgotten as their eyes widened. They exchanged appreciative grins and came toward her, but Kitty was able to elude them by running across the street and into a dark alley. She gave a cry as something soft brushed against her ankles. She jumped back and heard the startled plaint of a cat. She stood still and listened. Had they followed her? She shrank back against a building and waited, but no sound reached her. Staring down the twisting alley, she saw a light at the end. She had no recourse but to go toward it as quickly as she might. She picked up her skirts and ran the rest of the way, to emerge in a small square. To her utter relief and joy, there was a hackney coach standing only a few feet away from her, its driver huddled on his box and snoring loudly, while his horse, head buried in a sack, munched oats.

Kitty rushed over to it and cried, "Help me . . . help me, I pray you. I must get home."

"Eh, vat's this?" The driver lifted his head and stared blearily down at her.

"Take me home, please, please!" she begged.

"Can't do that," he mumbled.

"I pray you, please, I am lost!" she sobbed.

"Can't do that," he said stubbornly, "not until I knows where you're a-goin, Miss." He climbed down from his box, opened the door of the coach and helped her in. "Lord, Lord, you're a-shakin' all over. Shouldn't be out in this cold air vi'out a 'eavy cloak. You just tell me your direction, Miss, an I'll get ye there."

The sky was paling when Kitty finally reached her abode. Giving the surprised and gratified driver the two sovereigns which was all the money she had in her reticule, she hurried up the steps with his thanks ringing in her ears. It was several moments before a drowsy porter answered her frantic summons. She was so weary and upset that she could hardly make her way up the stairs. As she reached the landing near her chamber, Gareth suddenly appeared. He was wearing a long brocade robe and the candle he carried cast deep shadows on his face, rendering it strangely unfamiliar—even more unfamiliar because of the anger she read in his eyes. He strode to her and seized her wrist. "Where have you been?" he demanded in a low voice.

"I . . . I was lost . . . s-separated from Serena . . ." With a little gasp, she realized that she had actually forgotten the girl! "Is . . . is she here?"

"Yes," he rasped. "She is safely home—no thanks to you."

"To me?"

"Good God, Katherine!" His voice rose. He took her urgently by the arm and drew her into the dressing room that separated their chambers; setting the candle down on an adjacent table, he glared at her. "I have winked at your endless rounds of pleasure and your ceaseless extravagance. I have felt that as your husband I owed you something, but this last escapade passes all bounds of decent behavior! How dared you inveigle my sister into

155

an opera house masquerade—a veritable orgy? I pray it was ignorance and not wantoness that led you into this folly!"

"I . . . am thought to have inveigled . . . Serena . . ." she whispered.

"Do not attempt to deny it," he retorted sternly. "She told me how it was and how you left her and went off with David Vennor . . ."

"I did not leave her!" Kitty said hotly. "She would dance. I begged her not to go from the box, but she'd not heed me. After I was able to get away from David Vennor, I looked for her and I thought I saw Sir Nigel, but . . . but it was not he." She shuddered at the recollection of her ordeal. "And why would you think it was *I* who suggested this masquerade? I did not even know such things existed until she told me about it this morning!"

"Please," he said disgustedly. "I pray you'll not put it off on my sister. She told me how you begged, until against her better judgment, she relented and . . ."

"*Begged?* She said that? It's not true!" Fury welled up within her. "But you *want* it to be true, do you not? You want to believe the very worst of me so that you can go back to your Dillian with a clear conscience. I expect that with your strong sense of honor—that honor which prompted you to offer for me in the beginning—you find it difficult to put me aside without a good reason. So why not find me empty-headed, pleasure-loving and wanton, besides? As for my extravagance—I've not wanted to take money from you, but I thought it was my duty to look well as your wife, or would you have preferred me to go about in the rags I wore on shipboard? However, I might tell you that I had no intention of doing other than *borrowing* this money from you. I have written to my bank in America—I did it when I first came—and my

156

bankers here tell me I shall have my own resources upon which to draw within the week. At that time, I'll give you back every penny you've *squandered* on me. Nor need you worry about my remaining beneath this roof! I should go tonight—had I any place I *might* go—but as it is, I shall stay until my funds arrive, whereupon I shall set up my own establishment and then you may start proceedings for divorce—for you will be deserted by your bride! That should give you grounds enough, without disparaging my character. Indeed, I care not what excuses you use—I do not want to remain with a man who hates me because I am not the Honorable Dillian Vennor!"

She whirled away from him but her hopes for a speedy exit were flouted when she tripped over a footstool and fell heavily.

"Katherine!" He was at her side in an instant. "My poor girl, did you hurt yourself?"

"Go away," she gasped. "Go away and—and leave me alone." To her horror, she felt tears coursing down her cheeks. She did not want to weep before this man— but his unjustified accusations, arriving on top of all she had endured this night, proved too much for her—she was powerless to control the sobs that shook her.

"Katherine." He knelt beside her, pulling her into his arms. "If I have wronged you, I am sorry. My poor child, do not weep." Gently, he stroked her hair. "I—think there has been some manner of misunderstanding or . . . misrepresentation. Indeed, I am sure of it. Serena's not always very wise." He lifted Kitty and carried her into the bedroom. When he had set her down on the bed, he sat beside her, continuing to stroke her hair. "Come, my dear . . ." Gareth waited as her sobs lessened. "Hear me. I do not resent you. If only I were not in this damnable situation . . . If only I could *remember* . . . but no matter, I pray you'll not think of divorce; be patient just a little longer. Mayhap the fog will soon lift. Will you forgive me? I should not have misjudged you. I should have remembered, too, that Serena is a great one for shifting the blame from her shoulders, and also she's a bit of a madcap. I can see that the idea of attending a Masquerade at the opera house might have appealed to her. I was unreasonable, but I was worried about you, too—it is very late. No matter, I shall talk to my sister in the morning. There's no harm in her, you know. She is only headstrong, but she should not have laid the blame on you. That was unjust. Come, say you'll forgive me."

Kitty nodded. "I should not have . . . have . . ."

"Hush." Gareth's hand was in her hair again and, bending, he kissed her on the forehead. "You should go to sleep. You must have had a harrowing night. Here's Mary, come to put you to bed."

When Mary had left her, Kitty huddled down among her pillows, her eyes were dry and burning from her tears, but she knew that more would come. She was unable to hold them back. Gareth had been so like himself—so like the man she had come to love so desperately. Yet, though her great hope had been realized, though she had felt his arms around her—both the embrace and the kiss, she had coveted had been those of a friend, not a husband.

Nine

Five days wasted! Kitty sat at her mirror glaring at her image while Mary finished dressing her hair. She was pale enough for the abigail to have suggested a touch of rouge. Of course, she had refused, yet, as she surveyed herself, she wondered if it might not have been wiser to have accepted this aid. She looked wan and noticeably thinner. No wonder, since she had been confined to her chamber for the better part of a week due to the quinsy resulting from prolonged exposure to the chill winds in the drafty hackney coach on the night of the Masquerade.

Though she had chafed at this inactivity, she had been forced to abide by her doctor's advice. That gentleman, summoned when she had wakened late on the morning after her adventure with an aching head, chattering teeth and a swollen throat, had sternly inveighed against the foolish vanity of females who insisted upon mistaking early March for late May while braving its wintery breezes in the lightest of costumes. He had warned her against leaving her bed and, indeed, once he had dosed her with a most vile concoction, she had been too drowsy to do other than sleep for the rest of the day. It had not been until the third day that her head felt a little better, though still weak and groggy. Yesterday, her condition had been much improved and today, she could say positively that she was quite herself again: if she had entertained any doubts on that subject, they vanished immediately Mary had arrayed her in one of her new walking dresses. It was a round gown of a golden-brown merino which, when worn with a velvet spencer would be heavy enough to keep her warm. It was, she remembered, a French creation which had been very dear, but Gareth would not need to stand its expense!

On the second day of her illness, a letter had arrived from the bank, begging that Kitty call upon Mr. Sheffield at her earliest possible convenience, from which she inferred that her funds had finally arrived! She intended to make that call this very morning.

Even though Gareth had been both concerned and conciliating, Kitty was still determined to adhere to her decision to return whatever monies he had expended on her wardrobe. With that in mind, she had asked him for an accounting yesterday, only to receive an angry refusal and an injunction not to "make a cake of herself." Under the circumstances, she had not dared introduce the subject a second time. However, she would give him a lump sum and let him keep it or else deduct the proper amount from it. Kitty knew she would receive yet another argument, but she would not heed it! She exhaled an unhappy sigh.

During her illness, Gareth had been extremely solicitous, coming to see her at least five times a day, either sitting quietly beside her bed or, when she was feeling better, reading to her. His attitude had been warm and affectionate, but the affection and warmth were those of a brother, cousin or friend—anybody except a husband! Gareth had not, however, looked in on her this morning, and Mary had told Kitty that he had left the house long before she had awakened.

Kitty did not deceive herself as to the reasons behind that early departure. Undoubtedly, he had gone to see Dillian Vennor. Rather than arriving on the day she had expected, that elusive and tiresome girl had returned only yesterday.

Kitty had had this information from Serena, a most contrite Serena, who had mournfully explained that she had been jealous of David's attentions to Kitty and that was why she had come home without attempting to find her. Taxed with Gareth's denunciation of Kitty's "endless round of pleasure," the girl had weepingly admitted that she had deliberately encouraged her in this regard because she herself had wanted to partake of those diversions, formerly denied her by governesses and the companion who had chaperoned her until the advent of Kitty.

"I fear you will never forgive me," she had sobbed. "And nor will Gareth. He is furious with me on your account and because of my own actions. He has called me a 'handful,' and has suggested that I be exiled to the country again. It's all Nigel's fault—can you imagine that when he escorted me inside, he was still wearing his mask, pushed back over his brow. Of course, he had not expected Gareth would be waiting for me, but it *was* silly. I have been forbidden to see either him or David again because Gareth says they have encouraged me in my follies. Kitty, I pray you will forgive me. I am fond of

you, but it was so boring here . . . Yet I did not mean that
you should get into trouble and . . ." She would have
reiterated her contrition indefinitely had not Kitty responded, "Of course I forgive you."

She had brightened immediately. "Oh, that *does*
make me feel better! I do hope Gareth will relent on the
subject of David, otherwise it will make matters very
difficult when I see dear Dillian. I expect that she will
intercede for him and Gareth will relent once he's spoken
with her. I hope so for I miss him. He's not called, not
once since the masquerade."

It had been on the tip of Kitty's tongue to tell Serena
about her experience with David Vennor, but she had
thought better of it. It would have only aroused Serena's
jealousy—she might even accuse Kitty of having encouraged those most unwelcome attentions! And if she were
to tell Gareth, he might think it his duty to call David
out!

A knock at the door brought her musing to an end
and before she could answer it, Serena popped into the
chamber, her eyes gleaming with excitement. "My dear,
Kitty, you must come down at once! I have the most
delightful surprise for you."

"Surprise?" Kitty echoed. "What might you mean?"

"I shan't tell you, but I know you'll be pleased
beyond all measure—indeed, I am pleased for you, for I
can guess how much you have longed for this to happen."

Kitty started up. Her heart was pounding in her
throat. Could Serena mean that Gareth had finally recovered his memory? Was that why he had left the house so
early? Had he gone to consult a physician or . . . But to
waste time in idle speculation was useless. In a moment,
she would know.

Hurrying out of her chamber and followed by Serena, she sped down the steps expecting to find . . . she knew not what? She reached the hall, then stared about her confusedly. "What . . . where . . . ?"

"Kitty, my love." The voice, rich, warm, caressing, reached her from the threshold of the drawing room and brought her to a dead stop, as a tall man, clad in the latest fashion, strolled forward to smile broadly down upon her. "Kitty," he repeated emotionally, and reaching for her suddenly limp and nerveless hand, brought it to his lips. "At last, my dear little niece, I have been able to come and see you."

He was still holding her hand. She wanted to wrench it from his grasp—she wanted to strike the unctuous smile from his face, and order him from her presence; but mindful of Serena, the servants, and of the fact that she had no recourse but to welcome this man, whom she hated above all men on earth—save one—she said, "Rayburn, this is a surprise."

His smile grew even broader. "Why honey, if you aren't a sight for sore eyes. And all of us at home so worried about you. Addy was like to go into a decline."

A vision of his limp, bludgeoned figure being dragged out of her bedchamber was large in her mind. Under those circumstances, how could he face her so calmly—as if nothing had ever happened between them? She could not think of that. He had spoken of her mother. She had to know about Adeline. She had to ask, "Is Mama well?"

"Why she's just bursting with health. I am loaded with messages for you."

Serena interrupted, "I will leave you alone."

"Why that's right kind of you, Miss Quentin, but I hope I'll be able to see you again before I go?"

Serena blushed. "That would be my pleasure, Sir," she added shyly.

Seeing the blush and hearing a softened note in Serena's voice, Kitty recalled her arch look and her words concerning a "delightful" surprise. Obviously Rayburn had charmed the girl. She could not understand why. Though he was passably good-looking and certainly better dressed than usual, nothing could change his white eyes or the calculating look that was always in them—yes, even now. Kitty recoiled at the idea of being alone with him but there was nothing she could do save say pleasantly, "Will you not come into the drawing room, Rayburn?"

Once in the chamber, Kitty resented the appraising look Rayburn visited on the fine furnishings and such expensive trifles as a malachite box, several small perfect Meissen figurines in a boulle cabinet as well as the heavy velvet draperies and the crystal chandelier that centered an Adams ceiling. "Well, Kitty," he said as he took his seat opposite her, "I am right glad to see you so well-situated. I have been worried about you."

"Indeed?" she asked sarcastically.

He winced. "I expect you wonder how I had the effrontery to come see you, after our last . . . encounter. I can only say I was drunk and I might add that while I had a sore head for weeks afterward, I am glad I was stopped from doing you any harm. I damned deserved what I got. If I could've made amends, I would've done so. I hope you'll believe me. I hope, too, you believe I felt like a no-good hound dog when I heard what happened to you in Washington. I considered it was all my fault. If I hadn't acted as I did, you'd still be safe at The Oaks. But seems like I don't need to keep beatin' myself down any more, you being Lady Quentin and a Viscountess and all. All the same, I do hope you'll accept my apology."

It was her turn to wince, and she was glad that those strange white eyes could not see into her head and read the truth about her situation. It was possible, Kitty decided, that he meant what he said, though she doubted it. However, the past did not matter. Ironically enough, he was her one link with home—with her mother. She said, "I do accept your apology, Rayburn. As for what happened in Washington, none of that matters. Please, tell about Mama. You say she's well?"

"Well . . . and like I said, in the pink of condition. I note you do not ask about your brother."

"My brother!" Kitty exclaimed.

He looked at her in surprise. "Why surely you received Addy's letter about Jimmy—or rather James Wellington Farnsworth Abbott—to give the lad his full name."

"I . . . have a brother?"

"You most surely do . . . and you didn't get Mama's letter?"

"No, I—I haven't heard anything from her." Tears sprang to Kitty's eyes. "I have written and written . . . I thought she was sick or angry because of what Mrs. Heath might have said."

"Mrs. Heath." He shook his head. "That old hen sure did a lot of cacklin'; and so did that capon her son. Always told you he wasn't anything like a man, Kitty; but be that as it may, your Mama didn't set any store by what they said. She's received your letters and believes it happened just like you said it did. How could she, knowin' you, think you were a traitor and conspirin' with the enemy like Mrs. Heath put it? Wellington was like to have called Robert out except he knew he wouldn't go, mealy-mouthed coward that he is. I can't tell you how pleased I am that everything's turned out the way it has."

"You . . . are very kind," she said. "Please tell me more about Mama and the baby. Is he healthy?"

"He certainly is. Just think, Kitty, he was born on December twenty-fourth: a real Christmas present. By God, I have never been particularly fond of babies—but he is a beauty, yes, ma'am. Round and rosy. Great big eyes. Wellington says he has Addy's eyes and she says he's got Wellington's chin. Far's I can see, he looks just like himself, but if you really want to know about him, I have a letter for you from Addy and I am sure she has spent quite a few pages just going on about Jimmy. She was afraid you might not have gotten her letter, though she sent it to this house."

"It takes a long time for mail to arrive from America. Where is her letter?"

"Here it is." He reached into his coat pocket and brought out a large white envelope. Though she held out her hand, he did not give it to her immediately. "It's because of that letter I'm here. I guess you might call me your Mama's special envoy."

"Envoy?"

"It's about the terms of your Papa's Will, I've come, Kitty. Seems as if in the event of anything happening to your Mama, everything passes to you and your poor little brother's left out in the cold. Miss Addy's been fretting sorely about that. You know how much she loves The Oaks, and she thinks because she's spent the greater part of her life there, she'd like her little son to have some claim to it—along with you, of course. But 'specially now that you're living over here. Ever since Jimmy's birth, she's been talking about it. You know how she is when she gets a bug in her head—seems like she won't rest easy until she gets matters settled. However, I won't do any more talking about it—I'll let Miss Addy's letter speak for itself. I won't even stay around while you read it. I expect you'll want to be left in peace. But I would like to wait on you tomorrow, if that's convenient with you. Tomorrow . . . in the morning?"

She heard eagerness in his voice and there was a look in his eyes she did not like, though she was not sure why. Possibly it was only the fact that she had never felt comfortable with him—not even here where she was safe, where he could not follow her up to her bedchamber and attack her. Kitty wished she could tell him she did not want to see him again—but in view of how he had described her mother's state of mind, she could not do that. It was true that once Mama had her heart set on anything, she did not rest until she accomplished what she had set out to do. And must she give up part of The Oaks? It occurred to her that she did not want any child of Wellington Abbott's laying claim to her father's property. Was that selfish? He was her mother's child, too, her half-brother—James Wellington Farnsworth Abbott. Farnsworth had been the name of her maternal grandmother. She said, "Very well, you may wait on me tomorrow morning."

"At what hour?" He fairly shot the question at her.

"Eleven."

"Eleven, ah, excellent." Rayburn bowed over her hand and then held out the envelope. It was very thick. That pleased her; until that moment, Kitty had not even been aware of how very much she had longed to hear from her mother. She knew, too, that she would be willing to accede to anything Adeline desired of her—even though she guessed that Wellington Abbott might very well have persuaded her to make the request. In fact, now that she thought of it, she was sure that was what must have happened. She could hear her mother saying plaintively, "You know I never could abide strife, Kitty."

Half-sadly, half-amusedly, she smoothed the envelope; even to touch it was to bring Adeline back in the room with her.

As they came into the hall, Serena was tripping down the stairs. She gave a start as she saw them. Kitty swallowed a smile, guessing Serena's surprise to be feigned. Very likely, she had been up on the landing lying in wait for them—or rather for Rayburn. There was no doubt but that Serena had taken an immediate liking to him. "Oh," she said ingenuously, "I thought you must have gone, Mr. Abbott."

"I am leaving now, Miss Quentin." Rayburn smiled.

"Shall you be in London long?"

"Not long. We sail tomorrow or the next day, on the night tide."

"So soon!" Kitty exclaimed. "How can you reach Portsmouth in so short a time?"

"Oh, did I not tell you? I came on Wellington's yacht—the *Adeline*. She's anchored in the Thames."

"A yacht!" Serena breathed. "How utterly delightful."

"I didn't know that Wellington owned a yacht." Kitty was baffled.

"She's a recent acquisition—bought at your Mama's behest, the doctor having suggested that sea-air would be healthful for her."

"Then she's not well?" Kitty questioned quickly.

"Oh, yes, very well, a little peaked, perhaps, but for the most part blooming," he said easily. "I am sure she will have given you a highly detailed description of her condition in that letter." Rayburn added, "Perhaps you and your sister-in-law would like to come aboard the *Adeline*—this afternoon. I should be honored to have you as my guests."

"No," Kitty quickly remarked, mindful of her appointment at the bank. "It is not possible I have . . . a fitting."

"A fitting!" Serena exclaimed. "You said nothing to me about that."

"I expect I forgot about it—but I must go."

"Perhaps you will come to see the boat tomorrow," he said.

"Might we, Kitty?" Serena pleaded eagerly.

"Perhaps . . ." Kitty managed a smile.

"I shall live in hopes." He bowed. "Your servant, ladies."

When Rayburn had gone, Serena turned to Kitty. "Oh, he is so charming, and so very young to be your uncle."

"My uncle? He is not my uncle. He is the brother of my stepfather, and I must tell you that he is not as charming as you might believe."

"You do not like him?"

"No, I do not!" Kitty exclaimed emphatically.

"Oh." Serena nodded. "I expect I understand that. If my stepmother had had a brother, I do not imagine I should have called him my uncle; but you cannot expect me to entertain the same prejudices toward Mr. Abbott." Disappointedly, she continued, "I presume you will not wish to visit his yacht."

"No, I will not wish it," Kitty answered crisply.

"Oh, dear. I thought you would be agreeably surprised . . . but he mentioned a letter from your mother; you must be glad to have that. It's an ill wind, you know."

"Yes," Kitty agreed. "That at least is good."

Later, she was not so sure. It was a strange letter her mother had written—her handwriting was shaky and much blotted. The text of the missive had been discursive.

169

Of course, that was Adeline's way—but, at the same time, she had been oddly businesslike, and to say the least, uncaring of her daughter's feelings when it came to describing what she called a "fair disposition of the property."

Kitty perused the paragraph again.

> Of course, I quite understand your Papa's desire to leave the estate to you upon my demise. That was only natural since he had no other heirs.
>
> However, now that you are in England and wed to a nobleman with great estates of his own, I can imagine that you will find The Oaks only a burden. I expect that you will wish to sell the property—but before embarking upon this course, I beg you will consider dear little James. Though he is not your full brother, he is your close kin and born here in the same bed you were born, dear Kitty.
>
> I know you are not fond of Wellington—but would it not be better if the land were in the hands of your brother rather than that of a stranger, who would not have the love for it that he will have? I do not ask that you deed him the whole of it, but surely the house and the adjacent fields.
>
> Wellington assures me that the arrangements for such a transfer could be worked out quite easily—as you see I have included a document drawn up for me by dear Wellington's lawyer, Mr. Peebles, which I feel is very fair. It will give him the guardianship of James—in case anything should happen to me—though I am in much better health now than I have been in years—then when your brother is of age, the property will be turned over to him.
>
> Dearest Kitty, do not be difficult—do sign the agreement and give it to Rayburn—and let us all be peaceful.

Kitty frowned. She was extremely perplexed at her mother's reasoning. No one knew better than Adeline how very much her daughter loved The Oaks—had loved it ever since she was old enough to toddle around the house. She had a vision of its huge chambers with their elegant furnishings and many treasures—ivories and silks from China brought back by a seafaring Maynard. The table which had been a present from General Washington to her father, the fine volumes that Thomas Jefferson had given them from his own library at Monticello, the silver service made by Paul Revere, and the old Bible which had been the property of Sir Otis Maynard, the founder of the American branch of the family—a friend of Thomas West who had been governor of Virginia in 1610. There was more—so much more—but it was not only the beautiful house, which she loved, it was the ground beneath it. Adeline knew that, and yet she was asking Kitty to deed it to her baby brother, who was not a Maynard but an Abbott and stood to inherit Wellington Abbott's own plantation.

She could understand that her mother might want her son to live at The Oaks or even be its caretaker; and if she had asked her for her other properties, Kitty would have been glad to deed some of them to the boy, but The Oaks and its adjacent fields, the only home she had ever known—the only home she had, since it was impossible for her to think of sharing Gareth's properties or living at Ramsdale . . . .

That was another case in point. Her mother did not know anything about her present unhappy situation. Consequently, might she not think that Kitty must bring The Oaks as a dowry to her husband. Much as she had disliked Mrs. Heath, Adeline had always spoken about The Oaks and Heathlands being joined into one property when Robert and Kitty wed. Yet, here she was advising her daughter to give up the very heart of her holdings to the son of Wellington Abbott—though of course, Adeline would not think of him in that light.

"I need advice," Kitty murmured distractedly. Yet, whom could she ask? Gareth? She had never told him that she was an heiress—she had only told him why she did not want to return to The Oaks. If Kitty were to mention it now, he might think she was trying to bribe him into keeping the marriage together . . . but he had said he did not want divorce . . . That, however, must have been by way of comforting her or . . . She could not think of Gareth—it was too painful. His presence in her room these last days had it made it more painful and his absence was equally painful, for surely he was with Dillian Vennor. Kitty could not think of that, either; and tomorrow, Rayburn Abbott would be back for his answer —and why was he in such a hurry for it? Or possibly it was, as he had explained, Adeline who was hurried; Adeline who, in some way had turned against her daughter. Perhaps it was the joy of bearing a son at this late age when the doctor had assured her that she would have no more children. How pleased Papa would have been if . . . But again that was a painful thought. Yet she must talk to someone—a man of business . . . "Mr. Sheffield!" she whispered.

Not surprisingly, her projected visit to the bank had been wiped out of her mind by this letter. She jumped to her feet. If anyone could advise her, Mr. Sheffield could for he knew something of her affairs—his man had been told to look into them—and her funds must have arrived, and she could give Gareth . . . But that did not matter, either. Kitty uttered a dry little laugh; she was becoming as scatter-brained as her Mama, but, oh, she *would* like to see her—property or no property. And she was not jealous of little James, because her mother's health was better and that had been a nagging fear for months—she had looked so poorly when Kitty had left.

Purposefully, she went to the bell rope and rang for Mary. They must leave immediately.

"Brandy . . . fetch some brandy," Mr. Sheffield murmured distractedly. "I do not think the hartshorn was enough."

"There be no need, Sir, see, she's openin' her eyes."

"I never thought . . ." Sheffield began.

"Well, Sir, it were a nasty shock. Her ladyship's but recovered from a quinsy and the doctor did say she weren't to tax herself too much. Milady . . . Milady . . ."

Kitty, listening to the conversation above her, nodded. She could not trust herself to talk yet. She felt most miserably ill, and possibly she had turned blue; David Vennor had said something about turning blue after a swoon—when? The night of the masquerade? No, not then, long before and what did it matter when he had said it and why was she thinking about it now? Because she did not want to think about the news that Mr. Sheffield had just imparted to her, his manner not pompous at all, his eyes worried, as he had explained about Mama—Mama and the swelling which had not been a baby at all but a tumor, a malignant tumor, which had killed her mother months and months ago—so that she might not even have read the letter Kitty had sent her about her marriage to Gareth.

According to Mr. Sheffield, Adeline had fallen ill shortly after Kitty had run away. Was it her fault? Mr. Sheffield had answered that anguished question with a firm negative. Nothing could have saved her, that was what his informant had learned. Therefore the letter Kitty had meant to discuss with him was a forgery, part of a scheme to deprive her of The Oaks and deed it over to Wellington Abbott. The reason for Rayburn's hurry was thus obvious: soon other Americans would begin visiting England's shores and among them might well be people Kitty knew, who would console her for the death of her mother.

"I think we'd best give her brandy."

"No," Kitty whispered weakly, "I am myself again."

"Oh, Milady," Mary mourned, "I knew you shouldn't have come out."

Kitty made an attempt to rise and was quickly aided by Mr. Sheffield and his clerk; both men looked extremely concerned. "My dear Lady Quentin," the banker said. "I cannot tell you how sorry I am. If there'd been another way of telling you—"

She broke into his apologies. "I've not been myself, else I . . . I should not have been so disturbed." She could not bring herself to discuss the real reasons for her anguish; she could not tell him about Rayburn Abbott's forged letter; she had not the strength. "I—I must get home," she murmured.

"Yes, and immediately," Mary sounded almost stern.

The girl's attitude reminded Kitty of Jael, who would have been similarly stern, similarly protective. It was odd to recall that once she had actually disliked this young woman. Feeling as she did, it was pleasant to depend on Mary to help her from the bank and instruct the footman to lift her into the coach, the while scolding her gently for being too impulsive and getting up from her sick bed far too early. She had also offered her tearful condolences upon her mother's death.

"It do seem hard, and you so far away, Milady."

She had understood when Kitty had not wanted to discuss it. In a surprisingly brief time, Kitty was in her

174

bedroom again and though she had protested Mary's insistence that she swallow more of the doctor's ill-tasting medicine, it was a mercy to feel so sleepy; the encroaching drowsiness kept her from dwelling on Rayburn Abbott's perfidy in letting her believe that Adeline was alive and healthy—when in reality she was dead . . . dead . . . dead. . . .

Ten

When she awoke the next morning, Kitty had a confused memory of a dream in which she had heard Gareth crying out to her, "Kitty, Kitty, my own darling . . . listen to me." She had been so happy because in that dream he had not been the cold-faced stranger who called her Katherine, he had been the loving young man who had called her his "salvation." She had tried to speak to him but sleep had stifled her words and his image had wavered and changed into Mama, who was dead yet alive again, telling her softly, "Do not worry, Kitty, my love, all will be well, you'll see."

Tears stood in Kitty's eyes. She brushed them away angrily. *Nothing* was well. She hated dreams which promised so much and brought nothing but dashed hopes in the morning. Gareth did not love her, Mama was dead, and soon Rayburn Abbott like a great buzzard would be flapping his wings in the drawing room, waiting for her answer—the answer he hoped must cede The Oaks and its rich acreage to his brother! Well, he would soon find out that that was one more dream—from which the pair of them must needs awaken!

She pulled herself up against her pillows, thinking about their cruel deception. They could be apprehended as thieves but she would not do that. She did not want the whole county knowing how foolish and trusting Adeline had been—she was no Hamlet thirsting for her stepfather's blood—it would be revenge enough to see their elaborate schemes foiled. Let them go back to their scruffy plantation in Carroll County, if such a property existed. Perhaps it did not; perhaps they had lied about that, too; perhaps Wellington Abbott was nothing but a common trickster . . . She shook her head; it was a waste of time to indulge in useless speculation.

Sliding from bed, Kitty went to her desk and took out her writing materials. As she sat down, she was pleased to find that she was neither dizzy nor weak. She felt even better an hour later, as she re-read the note she had composed. It was quite the best of several tries, and she did not see how she might improve upon it. She had written:

Dear Rayburn:

After much soul-searching, I have decided that I must be selfish. I am too fond of my house and lands to give them up—even into the keeping of my half-brother. I am sure that when Mama thinks more about it, she will remember how I have always loved The Oaks.

Indeed, I have it in mind to spend part of my time there so that my children will know both England and

America and realize that they have an inheritance in each.

I will write to Mama at great length explaining my position and since you tell me she is in good health, do tell her Gareth and I shall be coming to visit her—probably in about two months' time. We are both looking forward to seeing the baby.

You will forgive me if I do not come down to say good-bye to you—I am not feeling my best this morning and my physician has said I must remain in bed. However, I do hope you have a pleasant voyage back to America. Please forgive me for my selfishness in this matter—but after all, James Wellington Farnsworth Abbott will inherit Abbott's Ford.

Again—my love to Mama and—as I said, I shall be writing soon.

Yours, etc.
Katherine Quentin.

She smiled grimly. To her mind it said everything and nothing. Undoubtedly, the fact that she had told Rayburn that she and her husband were coming to Virginia, must result in two sudden deaths—that of her mother and James Wellington Farnsworth Abbott. Meanwhile, she remained the sole owner of The Oaks. A wave of longing washed over her. She longed to see her home again, and she wanted to visit her mother's grave. If Gareth did not want her, if he agreed to a divorce—and he must, for she did not want to live with a man whose sense of duty was all that kept them together—she could go back to The Oaks and to Jael—and be Miss Kitty Maynard again.

In the early afternoon, Kitty, ignoring Mary's protests against her quitting her bed, acquiesced to Serena's suggestion that they drive in Hyde Park. Despite her grief over her mother, she felt wonderfully relieved that she had seen the last of Rayburn Abbott, without the necessity of having to speak to him.

It might have been better, perhaps, if she had sent the note to the *Adeline* thus sparing him the trouble of coming back to the house—but the idea of his arriving at eleven, full of hope that his scheme had worked, was too pleasant for her to ignore. Whoever had said that revenge was sweet had been quite right.

She had kept the note in her room until Mary arrived to tell her that Mr. Abbott was below. Then she had given her abigail the crested envelope. Dashing to her window, she had concealed herself in the draperies and waited for him to leave. He had taken a little longer than she had thought he must—probably he was so angry he had been momentarily rooted to the spot. She had almost expected he would demand to see her—but he had not. Finally, he had run down the steps. She had not been able to see his face, but she did not think that it was her imagination which told her that his back looked angry—rather than his habitual slouch, he held himself ramrod-stiff but his head had been lowered as he had climbed into the waiting carriage and was whirled away down the street.

She had a grim smile on her face as she envisioned Wellington Abbott's frustration when he learned of her decision. Unladylike epithets trembled on her lips as she thought of his duplicity. The brothers had been well-served by her. She would have been ecstatic, if it had not been for the thought of her mother's death—and Gareth. He had not come to see her this morning, either.

She recalled her dream; he had seemed to be with her, but of course he had not been. Dillian Vennor was home, and if he was not dancing attendance upon her, at least he was staying away from his wife—probably because it was becoming more and more difficult for him to remain in her presence. Well, he would not need to suffer it much longer, but she would not think of that either, not yet.

It was a lovely afternoon: the sky was blue and the park would be full of budding trees and early flowers As she started for the door, she caught a glimpse of herself in her long mirror. She was wearing the golden-brown merino she had donned yesterday and over it a dark green cloak trimmed with beaver. Her high-crowned bonnet was adorned with bronze-green cockfeathers. Amazingly, despite her ordeal, despite her interior miseries, she looked well. She did not hesitate to ascribe that to the fact that Rayburn Abbott and his brother were at last removed from her life. She did not need to think about them ever—ever again.

"Kitty," Serena called from the hall. "Are you coming?"

"Immediately," she answered. She was almost happy as she ran down the steps.

"Fool, fool, fool!!!!" Lying on the narrow bunk and hearing the river lapping against the sides of the ship, Kitty strained her wrists against the hard thin cords that bound them—but to no avail, they only bit the deeper into her flesh.

Because there was nothing else she could do, she thought on Serena's insistence that they drive to the Serpentine, where they could walk a bit.

"It will do you good," she had urged. "You've been inside for six days, you need some exercise."

Kitty had agreed and indeed it had been pleasant walking near that winding body of water that stretched through Hyde Park. Then, as they approached a clump of trees, Rayburn Abbott had suddenly appeared and fallen into step beside them and Serena, uttering a little self-conscious laugh had said, "I am sure you two have a great deal to say to each other." Before a shocked Kitty could remonstrate, she had disappeared among the trees.

Why, why, *why* had Serena drawn her into this trap?

Yet that did not matter. If Kitty had not betrayed the fact that she knew about his scheme, all would have been well. If she had been clever and answered his arguments with a polite disclaimer—a promise, perhaps, that she would reconsider her stand and possibly change her mind—if she had not called him a liar and a thief—but her impulsive temper had overcome her reason and she had contemptuously informed him that she knew the truth about her mother and "brother." Kitty winced as she recalled her fiery denunciation.

"If I chose, I could have you and your brother arrested as common thieves!"

He had responded by thrusting a pistol in her ribs and muttering that if Kitty did not come with him quietly, he would kill her on the spot. Of course, he never would have carried out that threat—he needed her signature on those documents, but she had been terrified and had submitted and now she was bound and gagged, a prisoner on board the *Adeline* and what would happen to her? She swallowed convulsively. The door opened and he stepped inside, his white eyes full of triumphant laughter.

"My dear, my *very* dear Lady Quentin," he drawled. "I am loath to have left your side for such a long time, but I had to make arrangements to sail. As I guess I explained to you yesterday, I wanted to leave either today or tomorrow; and now that my business is concluded to my satisfaction, I am going to be off on the night tide, as I think I also explained.

"I see that you have much you'd like to tell me, but unfortunately, I can't remove that gag—not yet. If you were to scream, they might hear you up on the riverbank and I could find that embarrassing. However, I am sure you must be interested in knowing what will happen to you. I suppose your little imagination is plumb full to the brim with ugly things like being shot or stabbed or even being fed to the fishes. Bless you, honey, I wouldn't do anything like that to you. I am real fond of you—I always have been, as I think I proved when I came into your bedroom that night.

"I was pretty disappointed not to have had my way with you, Kitty, love. All I had for my pains was a real bad headache, but I don't expect any headaches this time around. I can see by your expression that the idea of me making love to you doesn't appeal to you at all. But you'll be surprised how all-fired pleasant it'll be. Why I figure by the time we get back in an American port, you'll be eatin' out of my hand. Then we can get you a divorce and you'll marry me. I am rather sure your noble Lord won't put up a fuss. I expect he has too much pride to take another man's leavings—but me, I don't have any pride at all." He moved to the bunk. "My if you don't look pretty even with that gag stretched over your little mouth! You have lovely eyes, Kitty May, always thought so. You have lovely hair and a lovely body. I should like to prove my admiration to you at this very minute—but I expect I'll need to possess my soul in patience. However, once we're sailin' down the river . . ." He smiled. "I'll see you . . . all of you, Kitty May, tonight. It'll be dark before long, so I'd best make sure I've light to see you by. One of my men will be along with a lantern shortly; I'm afraid we don't run to gas lights on the *Adeline*." At the door, he bowed and went out, closing it softly behind him.

Tears she could not restrain ran down her cheeks—Kitty had no doubt that he meant every word he had said. But of course, he would not get his wish, because when he did free her, she would throw herself over the side of the boat. She did not want to die—but she would not want to live, if she were forced to suffer his touch, to endure his love-making. The very thought of it made her ill. If only she could get away . . . but she could not. If only someone knew of her plight, but only Serena knew and she would not tell.

Thinking on it, she should have realized that Serena was her enemy—encouraging her to be extravagant, telling her that Gareth approved of what he had later contemptuously described as her "endless round of pleasure." Serena had taken the blame for that on herself—but that had been a stratagem. It had all been part of a scheme to discredit Kitty, to make her appear empty-headed and frivolous. Why? Out of loyalty to Dillian Vennor, of course. Or perhaps it had been out of jealousy because David Vennor had pursued Kitty, and getting Rayburn to abduct her would remove her from both Serena's life and that of her brother. Had she really conspired with Rayburn to abduct her—no, Kitty did not believe that. There was no use trying to understand her motives . . . it had happened. Yet Serena might have second thoughts—but even if she did it would not matter. There were so many ships upon the Thames and no one knew where the yacht was anchored. Serena did know its name, but she would not help. . . .

Kitty glanced at the porthole; the light was dimming. It must be close on five in the afternoon or even later—soon it would be night . . . the night tide . . . and death.

The porthole had turned black, and Kitty was grateful for the feeble light of the lantern a dour crewman had set on a shelf across from her half an hour or so before. Soon they would be ready to cast off. Kitty, still straining against the cords that bound her, knew her wrists to be raw and bleeding. Odd how hope persisted when one knew all too well that there was no hope. It had been the same when it came to Gareth—all these months, she had hoped against hope that he would recover his memory. Well, there was far more of a chance that that would happen than that she would escape. The doctor had predicted it. And when he did remember, he would miss her and she would be gone. He might be saddened but he would recover, because Dillian Vennor was home and . . .

"Ahoy there, *Adeline!*"

Kitty tensed. Who had hailed the ship and why?

Why did she hope that it was someone come to rescue her? It was useless to hope. Undoubtedly, it was some official, someone from the docks, for some reason that had nothing to do with Kitty Quentin. Hoping was futile, unrealistic . . . but what was that angry cry?

"What's this . . . what do you all want?"

Was that Rayburn's voice? Or was it his captain or a member of his crew—cutthroats, the lot of them, probably. She had glimpsed them as she had been ushered board. They had been an ugly, hangdog lot. They had stared at her blankly—no, not all of them. Some had laughed and others . . . She did not want to think of the expressions she had surprised on their faces.

Feet . . . running feet on the deck. Surely that was unusual. She had not heard anything like that this long afternoon. She had heard voices, laughter, a ribald sea chantey. She had not heard running feet—but now she did . . . and shouting. Talking, too, in loud voices all at once, but she could make out an angry, protesting, "What do you mean? Why're the lot of you here? You got no right—"

Laughter. Excited laughter. It had never issued from

185

the throats of that crew. What could it signify? There was yelling over the laughter. Did she hear the sound of steel on steel?

"Where is she?"

Had she imagined she heard that? No. Was it still useless to hope that someone was looking for her? Was it wrong to tell herself she recognized the voice that had asked that question? Yes, that had to be a wild flight of the imagination. It could not have been Gareth's voice!

The door was suddenly thrust open—Rayburn strode in, his face a study in fury, his eyes wild—he looked like a hound that had gone mad at The Oaks; Kitty would not have been surprised to see white froth on his lips. He crossed to the bunk in what seemed a single step and grabbed her. She tried to struggle, but he held her too tightly. She had not known how very strong he was. He was muttering to himself or was it to her?

"They'll not find you, they'll not if I have to ... damn them, damn them, may they rot in ..."

They were outside—her face was pressed against his chest so that she could see nothing, but she felt a cold wind at her back—the night wind on which the ship would sail, but now ... perhaps not now, unless he succeeded in hiding her where they would not find her. If only the gag were not over her mouth. If only it would slip and she might call out—but it was tight, tight against her lips, bruising them. She could make no sound, not even when a hard metallic something was pressed against her forehead and Rayburn's loud, ugly voice close—too close—to her ear, was yelling, "One move from any of you and I'll spatter her brains on the deck."

She felt a cold, metallic pressure at her temple, and knew it with sick certainty for the muzzle of a pistol. She heard a click and knew he was cocking the pistol. Soon she would be dead.

There was a shattering explosion close to her ear and Rayburn's arms loosened. Kitty felt a wet warmth dripping on her cheek and knew she had been shot, though she felt no pain, only the warm liquid which must be her blood, running down her cheek. Someone had picked her up and was holding her in his arms. He was half sobbing, "Kitty . . . Kitty . . ."

She ought not to be able to hear that voice. She ought to be dead because the pistol had gone off, but there was no pain, and it sounded like Gareth's voice, but it could not be Gareth—he was calling her Kitty, not Katherine. She moaned deep in her throat because that was the only sound she could make with the gag pressed against her mouth. She wished to be able to speak, to utter some dying word. She must be dying—there was the blood, and her sight had already gone; she could see nothing. Why didn't the man who held her remove the gag? It would be only—but perhaps *he* could not see it, perhaps the darkness she was wrapt in was that of night only and not of approaching dissolution . . . .

She was being carried in her rescuer's arms—why did she persist in thinking that he was Gareth? There was a lot of noise around her—shouting and groaning. She was being lifted down, into a small boat, by the feel of it and yes, she heard the dip of oars and that voice which might belong to Gareth ordering them to row quickly.

"These ropes, they're so damned tight . . . damn him, *damn* him . . . and her wrists rubbed raw."

That voice, that agonized voice, did belong to Gareth. She wanted to tell him that it did not hurt—that nothing hurt anymore—but he had not removed the gag. He had cut her bonds and now his fingers were in her hair—he was pulling her hair—no, he was undoing the knots of the gag and it fell away.

"Gareth," she said. He did not hear her because *her*

voice was a mere whisper, but now it was louder, "Gareth," she croaked.

"Kitty, my darling, my darling, oh, my darling, oh my Kitty." His arms were around her. No need to question him, no need to say anything, just a need to let him hold her and feel his kisses on her upturned face and to vaguely hear men talking but . . . she could not listen to them, because the beating of his heart was loud against her ear and she was clasped very tightly in his arms and he was still calling her "Kitty . . . Kitty . . . Kitty . . ." *not* Katherine.

Kitty lay next to Gareth in the wide old bed she had never before seen, because she had been too proud even to look into the chamber that lay beyond her dressing room. Now she had seen it as he had carried her in there. He held her close against him and between kisses, he told her over and over again how much he loved her and how frightened he had been for her.

They had been lying there together for hours, and during that time she had heard how his memory had been stirring for the past week, how the illness she had decried had helped to restore it. Seeing her in bed, reading to her, had aroused vague images of himself lying in a bed, hurt. When he had read to her, he had seemed to hear her voice reading to him, hour after hour. Then he had gone to see Dillian Vennor, and found her looking as lovely as ever, yet her loveliness had meant nothing to him. She had seemed as remote as a portrait on the wall. She had told him she was betrothed and very much in love. He had congratulated her and come away relieved, because she had meant nothing to him. Seeing her had only stirred more memories of a little red-haired girl he had learned to love with all his heart.

"And I thought of your hands on my brow . . . you holding me close when Richard died, comforting me . . ."

He had been confused at first. He had walked for miles and miles around the city while memories had battered at his head and the past had mingled with the present and he had seen the extent of his unmeant cruelty to his wife—and feared that through that cruelty he might have lost her.

It *had* been his voice and not a dream, the previous night. He had come into her room, but had been unable to rouse her. The next morning he had gone walking again and on returning had been met by an anguished Serena, who had babbled out a story of being approached by Rayburn, with a tale of a misunderstanding between himself and the niece he cherished so fondly, and a plea for her to arrange a meeting to clear matters up. He had made out a good case for himself and Serena had obliged. When she had come back to the spot where she had left them, she had not found them. She had hunted for them, then thought they must have come home, but she had been frightened because it was so late.

"Rayburn Abbott. I remembered the name. I remembered you telling me why you did not want to go back to The Oaks—and then I went and collected some men from my old regiment . . . We searched for the *Adeline* and you know the rest."

She had not known all the rest. "What happened to Rayburn?"

Quite coldly, he had replied, "Someone shot him from behind, through the head, as he had threatened to do with you . . . and it was his brains that were splattered on the deck."

She had shuddered, and he had held her close until the shuddering stopped—until she was warm in his arms—until she had silenced his murmured apologies with her lips. She touched him now, just to assure herself that he was really there, and felt his arms tighten around her. Then, because she was so very weary, she fell asleep as she had once before in the cluttered attic of a house in Washington City.

The mirrored ballroom of Carlton House was brilliantly lighted. The air was heavy with the scent of roses set in huge baskets all along the walls. As usual, the Prince Regent had outdone himself in celebrating the recent announcement that his daughter Charlotte and her husband Prince Leopold were expecting a happy event. All of fashionable society was present and many of that brilliant coterie were whirling on the dance floor to the tune of one of the new German waltzes the Regent had introduced.

Standing to one side, their eyes on the dancers, were two young men, both garbed in the very height of fashion. Each had raised a quizzing-glass and both stared fixedly at a couple who appeared to have eyes only for each other.

"What I wish to know," one of the bucks remarked, eyeing the feminine half of the duo appreciatively, "is—but it cannot be true."

"I tell you it is quite true," his friend averred. "I have it from Lord Alvanley himself, who was present and witnessed the whole of the incident."

"She refused the Prince?"

"She refused the Prince."

"Good God."

"Precisely."

At that same moment, the other member of the duo, a handsome young man in well-cut satin evening clothes, looked at his partner, a bewitching lady of twenty-one, garbed in a gown of golden lace which complimented her russet hair and imparted a bright gleam to her laughing eyes. "Do you believe, my angel, that you were quite wise?" he demanded.

Kitty raised her green eyes. "I am sorry, Gareth," she said mendaciously, "but since it is our last night in London, I have told his Royal Highness that I wish to dance only with my husband. Oh," she added, "I am glad that you shall finally see The Oaks. Though I do wonder if I should leave little Gary in Mary's care?"

"She's proved a fine nurse and I think that at one, our son is a little young for an ocean voyage," he said seriously.

"I expect you are right," she sighed. "Why are you staring at me that way?"

"I was just thinking how beautiful you are. I do not believe I have ever seen you in such looks . . ."

"Oh, how you do run on," Kitty giggled. "That you can say that about a woman who has been a mother, and is expecting yet another addition . . ."

"*Another* addition?" he repeated amazedly.

"Oh," she laughed, "did I not tell you?"

"You did not!" Gareth said sternly and came to a dead stop, only narrowly avoiding being hit by an indignant couple.

"Why are we stopping?" she inquired. "The music's just begun."

"You know why," he chided. "You must rest, and how can you even contemplate an ocean voyage? We must defer our plans."

"Defer our plans? We could not . . . Serena and David would be devastated. You know they count this as their wedding trip."

"Your health comes first."

"I think I ought to have explained, my darling ... it's not for another eight months."

"Ah," Gareth grinned. "In that case ..." He made as if to whirl her back into the dance, but instead, bent down and kissed her.

"Well!" A dowager darted a shocked glance at the woman sitting next to her at the edge of the floor. "Such untoward behavior, and with his own wife! And you say she refused the Prince? I really can't understand that."

"The explanation's quite simple," her friend replied. "She's an American, my dear."

"Oh." The dowager stared in the direction of the pair who had rejoined the dancers once again. "An American. I see. Well, that does explain ... *everything.*"